THE POSTIE CHRONICLES

DIARY OF A POSTIE
(EDITION 2)

By

Glenn Thompson

Glenn Thompson

Copyright © 2026 Glenn Thompson

All rights reserved.

No part of this publication may be reproduced, stored in a retrieval system, or transmitted in any form or by any means, electronic, mechanical, photocopying, recording, or otherwise, without the prior written permission of the copyright owner, except for brief quotations used in reviews or scholarly work.

Table of Contents

Glenn Thompson

Foreword

"It's a state of mind. It's that place where you lose yourself and you find yourself." – 'Bodhi' (Patrick Swayze, *Point Break*, 1991)

Ever since I watched that classic movie back in '91, when I was 21, that line from the late, great Patrick Swayze, or rather, 'Bodhi', the surfing Zen Master, stuck with me. Of course, he was talking about wave riding and the endless search for the perfect wave; sort of like life in general, and the search for solace, peace of mind, or perhaps both.

I likened it to my own personal quest, which began in childhood and extended into my early adult life, particularly the search for a vocation: to earn a dollar, to pay the rent, but most importantly, to find something that agreed with my daydreaming mind.

The lyrics to the song by Australian music icons Men at Work, *"Be Good Johnny"*, typified my mindset: "I only like dreaming, all the day long…"

That was me at school. And it didn't end there, it followed me into my first working years as a young adult. I suppose I was looking for a job that allowed my mind to drift into another stratosphere while still achieving the desired result at the end of the day. Yep, I was searching for something as rare as rocking horse shit.

I never wanted a 'real' job, or one that consumed my mind. I wanted something I could leave at work when I clocked off, something that wouldn't keep me awake at night as I pondered how I could have done it better earlier that same day. And I absolutely despised the idea of a boss constantly looking over my shoulder.

It took me until I was 23, almost 24, to finally find it. I had a light-bulb moment, made a phone call, rode my pushbike 10 km to an interview, and over the Christmas period of 1993, I was casually employed as a pushbike postie. Three months later, it became a full-time job.

The freedom of being a postie, particularly in those early days, is something I look back on with fond memories, and I found myself itching to go to work each day, believe it or not. And I never once took the job home with me; it was one of those jobs that stayed exactly where it needed to stay: at work. And no one looking over my shoulder.

You following me so far?

I spent most of my adult working life as a postie, you know, the one who gets chased by dogs while riding a motorbike or pushbike during mail deliveries. (That was my first impression of the job, too.) As it turned out, there were a few more twists and turns than that initial first impression, so I decided to write this book to explain them in detail.

Postman, post lady, post person, mailman, mail lady, or delivery officer, no matter what form of transport they use, whether on foot, pushbike, motorcycle, van, or the new electric vehicles, the most common and endearing term has always been, and probably always will be, the postie.

I wrote a diabolical, rough first draft of this book during COVID because I was bored. I slapped it together and self-published it on Amazon. It was more about the fact that most of my fellow workmates kept telling me I should do it (because I was always talking about how one day I would) and many also telling me I would never do it, but the idea had merit anyhow.

Perhaps it was more about appeasing some and proving the rest wrong. Either way, the final product was, in a word, ordinary, with enough errors to rival a primary school kid's first story-writing effort.

So, I decided to rewrite it properly, to do the book, my fellow workmates, and the job itself some justice. If you do find some errors this time around, apologies once again. (Hey, there are probably a lot fewer errors than in my initial effort.) But I am no writer, in all seriousness.

I've simply done my best with the limited ability I have as a budding author. If you're looking for a Tim Winton-style book, full of descriptions that sound as though they've been plucked straight from a Walt Disney movie, this definitely isn't it.

I was once told by a fellow workmate, "As far as writers go, GT, well, you're a pretty good postie." That basically sums up my writing, I guess. The whole idea of this book is simply to explain the job in detail, and perhaps offer an insight into how the postal industry in the land of Oz works, without getting myself sued in the process. Without blowing my own trumpet too much, I reckon I may have covered most angles reasonably well.

(Not sure about getting sued yet; give it time.)

I should add, most of this book focuses on the experiences of a postie delivering mail on a Honda 110 motorcycle at a place I will simply refer to as 'The Post Office' in Western Australia, although my final seven years in Oz Post were spent delivering parcels in a van on the south coast of WA.

(A change is as good as a holiday.)

Here it is:

The Postie Chronicles (Diary of a Postie, Edition 2)

Chapter 1:
Customer Profiles

I felt it necessary to start this book with some customer profiles because, let's face it, that's basically the job in a nutshell: delivering to and meeting all kinds of customers. Please don't be offended if one of the following profiles fits your description. Rather, take it as a compliment, you left a lasting impression on me.

If you don't find your profile in Chapter 1, don't despair; I've added plenty more throughout the book. Otherwise, we probably wouldn't have got past the first chapter, as there are obviously quite a few different personalities out there in suburbia.

The 'WTF HAS SHE ORDERED NOW?!' Customer

If I had a dollar for every time I used to hear, "What the f... has she ordered now?!" I reckon I'd be a very wealthy man.

It was usually a comment from the bloke of the household as they answered the door to the knock of their local postie, only to find the item being delivered was for their better half. However, take it on good authority, there have been plenty of males I've seen over the years who had an online shopping habit that went well beyond their quota.

It wasn't just a one-way street, by any means.

Online shopping, let's face it, is ridiculously easy, and a lot simpler than getting in the car and driving to the local shopping centre. It's a part of everyday life now, though some take it to different levels of enthusiasm.

I recall some weeks where the 'usual suspects' would receive goods almost every day, and I got to know those customers well. They were always happy to see their postie, and it was a win/win. Let's face it: happy customer, happy postie, happy days.

The problem with some households, however, was obvious: not everyone was informed of the incoming goods, which could create a bit of conflict, usually light-hearted, particularly if the financial aspect of it impacted the weekly budget.

As an online shopper, particularly if you're in a relationship, I reckon it's a good idea to inform your other half of incoming purchases. It saves not only possible conflict but the ensuing interrogation that many posties witness daily on their rounds.

(Personally, I found it most entertaining.)

Yes, it's possible to hide an online purchase. If your work hours differ from your partner's, and if all the planets align, your order may go relatively unnoticed, letting you escape the backlash that occurs when communication hasn't been adhered to.

However, always allow for the planets *not* to align, and for your other half's day off to occur when you least expect it.

"What the f... has she (or he) ordered now?!" can always be avoided by thinking ahead: get it delivered to your work address and tell your boss, "It's a gift for my other half, and I didn't want to risk them receiving it at home."

As the saying goes: work smarter, not harder.

The 'Ghost' Customer

Whether on bike or van deliveries, this one always made me feel very uncomfortable, and it was quite remarkable how many times it occurred.

Upon reaching an address, I'd often have my back turned to the property while searching for an item on the back of my bike or in the van. Within what seemed like seconds, someone would appear almost out of nowhere.

Yet they hadn't spoken or made a noise, they just stood there and stared.

"Geezers, you scared the shit outta me, mate!" I once said to a bloke who did just that. He appeared out of nowhere, said nothing, and just stared. And yes, he scared the shit out of me.

As I located his parcel and handed it over, he thanked me and walked off. I never knew whether he was just a quiet sort of chap, or whether he was, in fact, a ghost. He had all the attributes of one, as far as I was concerned.

If you're one of those customers who like to scare the postie, a simple "G'day mate" wouldn't go astray.

The 'Shy' Customer

There are plenty of shy people in this world, and sometimes I liken them to the ghost customer. I've witnessed them more than once.

The scenario usually plays out like this: arriving at a letterbox on the Honda 110, I'd see someone move behind a tree to completely block themselves from view.

I remember once calling out, "Hi there, I have a letter for you!" Nothing, no reply.

Sometimes it almost resembled a scene from an eerie movie, where you thought you saw some movement, then question whether you saw anything or anyone at all. I've often looked back to see someone briskly walking from behind the tree to the letterbox.

Personally, I've never taken offence to that type of customer; some simply don't wish to see the postie, just their goods. We're all different, and I'm living proof of that.

The 'Aggressive' Customer

I once had a customer snatch mail from my hand and look at me as though I'd handed him a summons to court. Perhaps I had. Either way, he was no little ray of sunshine, and he certainly wasn't happy to see me. He glared like a drunk patron would in a pub after too many beers if you dared look in his direction.

"You wanna go, maaaate??"

OK, he didn't say that, but that was the impression I got. He was the complete package: black tee-shirt, tight denim jeans, tattoos, and a face only a mother could love.

I remember our team leader at 'The Post Office' telling me on day one: "If anyone gives you a hard time, just tell them to have a nice day."

So that's exactly what I did, and I still think to this day that I totally confused him. As I rode off, I remember the look on his face, like a confused puppy, complete with the head tilt.

I had a brief moment in my mind of Bon Jovi singing their classic hit, *"Have a Nice Day"*, which is really all you can say in a situation like that when an aggressive customer gives you attitude. As a postie, it's up to you whether you're confident enough to sing it, but I'd always recommend saying it as it softens the moment, so to speak.

During van deliveries, I had a customer have a go at me for knocking on his back door instead of the front door, though there was a valid reason. His front gate was locked and blocked by two garbage bins, so I followed a side driveway that led straight to the back door.

I naturally knocked first and called out, "Anyone home?"

He came out with a full head of steam and asked why I hadn't gone to the front door. I explained that usually I would, but due to the locked front gate and the side driveway leading directly to the open back door, I didn't think it would be an issue. After he signed for the parcel, he slammed the back door on his way in.

You can't please every customer all the time.

The aggressive customer is alive, unfortunately well and should be avoided where possible. When in doubt, tell 'em to *have a nice day*.

The 'Deaf' Customer

This type of customer is always difficult to gain a signature from if you're a postie, due to the obvious, they can't hear much. When I say deaf, I mean it in two respects: one, medically deaf; the other, simply didn't hear the postie when they knocked on their door.

Deafness is a fact of life, and I mean that with no disrespect. However, blaming the postie for not knocking when they in fact did is most frustrating, believe me. Regular complaints filter through the postal industry about a customer receiving a card rather than the goods, though one thing can be assured: if a customer finds a card wedged in their front door, it usually spells one thing,

The postie *did* knock before writing out the card.

Given the many things that can go on inside a household on any given day, it's highly possible someone may have been in the shower, out in the backyard, in the toilet, listening to loud music, or even enjoying an intimate liaison. So if a card is found at the front door, at least give the postie the benefit of the doubt.

Personally, I have never gone all the way to a customer's front door to write out a card without knocking, as there would be no point. I *always* knocked as well as rang the doorbell as many doorbells don't even work and are simply there for show.

If I could offer some friendly advice to a customer, it would be the following: if you find a card on your front doorstep or wedged in your door, rest assured the postie made an effort to find you. Ringing through a complaint will always be met with the same answer by the postie to management:

"Well, I did knock, Boss, they obviously didn't hear me."

End of argument.

The 'Near Naked' and 'Fully Naked' Customer

When I first started my career as a postie, some of the stories from the older guys were priceless regarding near-naked or fully naked customers going about their business at home as though they were the only person there.

Well, technically they were, until the postie knocked on the door. Yet that rarely changed the way they dressed, or rather, undressed.

A parcel contractor once told me about a woman who came to the door straight from the shower, and the towel came off, but she had no inhibitions and acted as though nothing had happened while signing for a parcel.

So, did I ever experience a near-naked or fully naked customer in twenty-something years of delivering goods? Yes, of course I did, several times, law of averages. Sometimes it can be a bit of a letdown, depending on your personal preference.

I used to regularly deliver to a house where a bloke of around 70 years would answer the door in his jocks, showing zero inhibitions. I'd always think to myself as I rang the bell: *Just keep eye contact, buddy. Don't look down...*

Here's a rather comical twist to this story: the jock-wearing gentleman shared the same surname as a local businessman. On a delivery, I asked the obvious question: "Mate, your dad wouldn't happen to live about 10 minutes out of town, would he?"

He replied, "Aah, yep. What's he done now?"

I described the regular attire he wore when answering the door, and he said:

"Yep, that's dad alright. Lucky you, buddy, sometimes he comes to the door wearing nothing!"

(Lucky me indeed.)

Some customers are completely in tune with nature and oblivious to anyone else when answering the door. Being a postie has its advantages *and* disadvantages. Perhaps the job can be likened to that famous Forrest Gump quote: *"Life is like a box of chocolates, you never know what you're going to get."*

The near-naked and fully naked customers can either drag out the signing process or speed it up to record time.

"G'day mate, parcel at the door for you, have a ripper day."

"You don't want me to sign?"

"Nah mate, scanner's not behaving itself, I'll sort it, gotta run."

The life of a postie can be seriously entertaining, trust me.

The 'Adult Film Scene' Customer

Now come on, seriously? Nope, it never happened to me in my postie career. But somewhere out there in the land of adult movies, there's quite possibly a scene resembling this. I've heard occasional stories about customers taking a shine to their postie, and things escalating, but it didn't happen in the 23 years I spent with Oz Post.

As far as a bit of 'loving during delivery time' goes, yes, I've been fortunate enough to be counted among the 'lucky' ones.

I received a message one morning while sorting mail from a lady I was seeing at the time. Her text read:

"Hey Mr Postman, how's ya day looking?"

(She always called me 'Mr Postman', just like the song by The Marvelettes from 1961.)

I replied something along the lines of: "Yeah, not too bad, perhaps a 2 pm finish."

She replied: "I have a lunch break at 12 pm."

That's when my mind went into overdrive. It wasn't as though she'd even mentioned food, so I replied with the obvious:

"My shack, 12 pm it is."

As a postie, if you know you're going to lose 30–45 minutes of delivery time because of a 'better offer', it's necessary to up the ante with sorting. That day, after her message, I moved into another gear with the mail because it wasn't an overtime day, I had to be signed off by around 2 pm.

If I'd gone into overtime, it probably wouldn't have been the end of the world but management may have questioned why I was out there so long.

I went through the rest of the sorting like a shark on a feeding frenzy and got out of the office with time to spare. Long story short, I made the 12 pm lunchtime and the 2 pm finish deadlines, and perhaps fitted the description of this post in a strange sort of way.

Not exactly a Hollywood or adult film scene, but hey, near enough sometimes is good enough.

The 'ALL CLEAR!' Customer (Weekend at Bernie's)

The term 'All Clear!' reminds me more of a fellow employee than anyone else. However, I've met a few customers over the years who shared the same trait. My good buddy Wal and I used to quietly take the piss out of a workmate who basically needed a defibrillator to shock him into action. If he were any more relaxed, he'd have been asleep.

Relaxed is probably the wrong terminology; 'the lights are on but nobody's home' is more accurate.

Not everyone is lively due to things going on in their lives. But some customers (and workmates) simply choose to be like 'Bernie' and show very little life whatsoever.

If you haven't seen *Weekend at Bernie's*, do yourself a favour. It's about a bloke who died, but visitors got around that inconvenience to enjoy his mansion for a weekend so they kept him alive, sort of.

I've met several customers with the same traits as Bernie, who might have required a defibrillator to inject life into them. When delivering to these types, I usually found the best way was to do it quickly as they usually weren't interested in conversation, just their item.

Once again, I'm not criticising anyone with medical or age issues, it's more about those who simply choose to be lifeless and show no real emotion or gratitude.

'Bernie' and the 'All Clear!' customer are alive and well (although sometimes debatable) and are generally just going through the motions. I'm fairly certain to this day they just didn't like me personally, hence their lifeless attitude towards me.

You can't please everybody.

The 'I'm Too Busy' or 'Too Important' Customer

This type of customer is too wrapped up in their own little world or feels too important to acknowledge the postie and it always bothered the shit out of me to be honest.

For example: I've delivered a non-signature item to a front door, knocked, scanned it, and left it in a safe spot. Sometimes I've even seen the customer inside through a flyscreen door and called out "Parcel!" before heading back to my van or bike.

I've looked back to see the recipient glance at the item, make eye contact with me, grab it, and walk back inside, without the slightest acknowledgment.

Sometimes I would talk to myself as I headed back to the delivery vehicle…: *"…and thank you, postie, have a nice day…"*

You know the situation, you've probably done it yourself a few times in life.

Sometimes the customer may have been on the phone, but it only takes a second to yell a quick "Thanks, postie!"

If you're one of those customers too busy (or too important) to do that, c'mon, you're better than that. I know it, you know it.

Unless your postie is a complete nitwit, and you really don't like them personally (which I doubt), they deserve a bit of thanks for safely delivering your item.

It doesn't take much…

The 'Dancing' Customer (Anna)

I promised this particular customer that I would include her in this book—if, of course, I ever wrote it—which obviously I now have. So here she is: *Anna, the Dancing Customer.*

I used to have a regular habit on my van deliveries of perhaps playing my music a little too loud. I'd immerse myself in my favourite tunes whilst out on deliveries, and I think it helped with my work ethic as it basically kept me vibrant—or perhaps even a little 'hyped up'.

One address I used to regularly deliver to was a safe distance out of suburbia, and I suppose that when I was out of earshot of the general public, I'd give the volume a few extra notches on the van stereo, which was hooked up to my iPod Shuffle.

Def Leppard was generally my tune of choice, as I love a bit of glam rock.

When I first commenced my deliveries to Anna (I think that was her name), I'm uncertain how long it took for her to start the dance moves, but it became commonplace after a while. She'd hear my music— probably from a distance away—and by the time I pulled up at her house, she was already into her dance moves routine, making her way down the front path.

I've never witnessed anything quite like it on deliveries.

Anna was a joy to deliver parcels to; in fact, if ever I saw a parcel for her during early morning sorting, I'd just hope that she was home. It was always a bit of a letdown when she wasn't, as she brightened up my day with her energy.

Anna, if ever you read this book, I hope you're still rocking the dance moves for your new postie. It was an absolute pleasure to have delivered to you, and if the world had more customers like you in it, well, the world would be a better place—particularly for the postie.

The 'Obscure Item' Customer

Whilst I generally never had much of an idea as to what items most customers had ordered, some were pretty easy to work out—things like baseball bats, for example. Some items filter through the postal system with a description printed on the packaging, such as *'adult toys'*, which, believe it or not, come through regularly.

These 'toys' are simple to decipher as they have a distinctive shape and length to them, so when a postie sorts the item, it basically *stands out*, for want of a better description. I apologise in advance—the following story is *not* about an adult toy; I was simply giving an example.

I encountered a rather strange item on parcel deliveries a few years back that had me scratching my head as to how you could even find something like that on the net. The whole situation came to light through a stolen item incident.

I'd left a safe drop item on a doorstep behind a pot plant and the item got stolen; this was explained to me by an elderly customer the following day, as I had another delivery for her. The day the item was stolen was her shopping day, and perhaps someone was aware of her movements and then watched me stop at her house and drop the goods off.

After she gave me a bit of a rundown on the situation, I offered my apologies, which she wouldn't accept, stating that it wasn't my fault—more so a case of bad timing than anything else.

"Sincere apologies—was the item expensive?" I asked.

This was her response:

"No dear, it wasn't. It was a lining for a drawer—you know, the ones that hold your knives and forks, etc.? Well, that's all it was, so don't stress. A plastic lining I ordered from overseas, and it cost me about three bucks."

It got me thinking (once again).

That customer pretty much went online to find something as obscure as a drawer liner, and despite the fact that it got stolen by some peanut—who would have been well and truly disappointed with the contents of the heist—it was something that probably cost more to ship from overseas than to buy locally. Yet, it's the world we live in, and it's why posties will always have a job, despite the fact that one day the letters side of deliveries may become totally obsolete.

To the peanut who stole the item—just in case you ever read this book—how's that drawer liner going, champ? And did you put it to good use??

Chapter 2:
Mrs Smith and Karen,
Postie/Customer Interaction

Thirty-three years have now passed since I was fortunate enough to stumble upon what would become not just a new career, but an outrageously enjoyable way of life, like the surfers in *Point Break* who were living the dream in that cult movie.

Becoming a postie afforded me time outside of work to have a life, to hit a golf ball, to continue teaching tennis and, most importantly, to spend time with my three kids. While I was at work, however, let's just say it was a ridiculously enjoyable environment to earn a wage, due mainly to the guys I worked with.

I suppose it's fair to say that many day-to-day experiences, not just on delivery, but probably more so in the office, I took for granted, as though they would simply keep occurring. In all seriousness, they did.

One thing I never took for granted, however, was the customer, the person responsible for my job, the reason I was employed from day one. However, as I've written on more than one occasion in this book, some were more enjoyable to deliver to than others.

I developed some lifelong friendships with people who relied on me to get their goods to either their front door or into their letterboxes. I met some ripper customers, and some I used to cringe at seeing. However, I'm stating the obvious when I say that without the customer, good or bad, a postie does not exist.

I often liken customers to two people who I'll write about in more detail as the book goes on, *Mrs Smith* and *Karen*. One is a joy to deliver to, and the other is the face of what's wrong with today's society, well, in my humble opinion anyhow.

Being a postie is really all about making sure the customer receives the item addressed to them with a minimum of fuss, and I guess it's up to each individual whether they do it with a smile, but I think it helps.

Those items may be in the form of a personal letter, a utility bill, a magazine, a legal document, an ordered item from Amazon, or, in the case of the van driver, it may be something as unique as a box of insects, which pet stores order from time to time.

Yes, insects. Certain reptiles have to eat too.

I vividly recall my early days of delivering predominantly letters on a pushbike, and it occurred to me that it was a win/win type of job. By that I mean that Mrs Smith was always thankful when her postie stopped at her letterbox while she was perhaps in her front yard watering her garden.

"Good morning, Mrs Smith, how are you? Sorry, not great news, got a bill for you."

Personally, I hated delivering utility bills, particularly to customers as nice as Mrs Smith, but it was all about how you did it and, on most occasions, I'd apologise first, which was always met with a laugh if they had a sense of humour.

Hey, it's like anything really, as inevitable as death and taxes, two things as common as receiving a utility bill. It's up to the customer how it's received, but most would offer a gesture of gratitude regardless of what I delivered them.

You see, it didn't matter what Mrs Smith received; she was simply grateful that her postie had something for her. It was someone she could have a chat with, to break up the day, a conversation with a stranger basically, if the postie was new to her area, but someone she'd get to know and trust over time.

If I had a bill for an aggressive type of customer, then I'd just pray in advance that they weren't in their front yard at the time so I could simply slip it in their letterbox and keep moving. I was always told from the start that if ever I saw a customer in the front yard, to hand-deliver their mail rather than ignore them and just place it in the box.

Customer relations, made sense really.

Not long after I started as a postie, I attended a course at my local post office where a Zen Master of the industry arrived to deliver the gospel, to reiterate what we'd all been told from day one on the job:

"Look after the customer because without them, you don't have a job."

Wise words of wisdom, but pretty obvious all the same. Sometimes it helps, though, to spell certain things out to not only new employees but seasoned ones also, to reinforce basic work ethics.

I vividly remember the job being described to me by a particular gentleman in a way that's stuck with me ever since:

"Remember, guys and girls, when the postie is seen delivering up and down the streets of suburbia, to many people it's a sign that everything is still OK in the world."

It got me thinking, he was very correct. Mrs Smith may not have been happy with her bill from Telstra, yet the postie made her day by simply being there, because he or she is a symbol of what's still good in the world. You know, the simple things in life. (I'm not calling a postie simple, but I think you know what I mean.)

I recall another guru of the postal industry talking about Mrs Smith and the way she talks about not just *the* postie, but *her* postie.

It's a fact of life that customers get attached to people who regularly have something to do with their everyday life, and that can be traced back to times when the milkman used to do the rounds in the wee hours of the morning. Just like the postie still does, and just as the old-school milkman once did, he or she offers a service that customers get used to and, in some instances, they're considered part of the family.

I can still remember the days when I was a kid and the garbage truck would drive up and down our street with a couple of guys hanging off the back of it who'd jump off at each property, grab the bin and empty the goods into the back of the truck. At Christmas time, we'd leave a bottle or two of beer out for them as a small token of our appreciation for taking our rubbish away over the course of the year.

Those guys, well, they were *our* garbage men, and part of *our* family, who we'd have the occasional chat with as they disposed of our rubbish. And even though it was only once a week, we looked forward to seeing them.

It's a privilege to be someone who's often embraced by a customer (not physically, though I've heard stories from fellow workmates). In the case of the postie, although some may take it for granted, it's a job that can deliver a good vibe back to the delivery person themselves.

Mrs Smith is still saying thank you for her bills and, according to many (particularly her), the world is still a good place to be when the postie rides, drives, or walks up and down the streets of suburbia.

Long live the postie, and long live Mrs Smith.

'Karen'

Whilst Mrs Smith has long been portrayed as the perfect recipient of addressed goods, and the one who all posties love delivering to, the changing face of society has now installed *Karen* as someone just as influential in customer deliveries, though for all the wrong reasons.

Karen is the name given to a customer who's usually unhappy with not just her postie, but the world in general, so she'll constantly be making complaints about someone she considers to be a public nuisance.

Urban Dictionary states the following in regard to her:

Karen is 44, and a mother of three. Blonde, owns a Volvo, annoying as hell and wears acrylics 24/7. Currently at your workplace speaking to your manager.

So you see, Karen is in fact real, she's made the pages of a dictionary. However, I sincerely offer my apologies to you if your name is Karen and you're a little ray of sunshine. My eldest son has seen it all, he used to work at a retail store and dealt with Karen on a regular basis, he tells me.

As far as complaints to postal management go, well, they vary. However, one in particular upsets Karen more than anything else, and she'll deal with the issue the only way she knows how: publicly. The most common one is when a postie writes out a card for a customer rather than knocking on the door to gain a signature for an item, as he or she has assumed that the customer wasn't home when in fact they *were* home.

In the postal industry, it's commonly referred to as a *shortcut*, to save a bit of time here and there. (Not the smartest move a postie can make, but it happens.)

True story for you: I was called into the boss's office a few years back regarding a parcel delivery that I apparently made *no attempt* to deliver. The customer sent through a complaint stating that I'd bypassed her front door and also claimed I'd left a card in her letterbox when I'd actually wedged it in the front door.

Modern technology is a wonderful thing, however, and can be your friend at times. My scanner held a reflection photo of me standing at her front glass door, where I took a photo of the card I'd left for her after she didn't answer the door when I knocked.

Not guilty.

(More on scanner photos later.)

Now, YouTube is a wonderful part of the internet as we all know, and it's a great way of finding just about anything you require, from how to fix something, to how to cook something, to how to publicly humiliate someone.

Yes indeed, YouTube is your one-stop shop.

Unfortunately, several posties have become famous, or rather *infamous*, particularly amongst their workmates, for doing something that's upset Karen. She's shared their exploits on social media for all to see. Those posties have their very own section on YouTube titled *Posties Not Attempting Delivery*, uploaded by a Karen or two.

We've all attempted a shortcut in our lives, whether at work or at play, and let's face it, a shortcut can save a bit of time on a busy day. However, the ensuing paperwork from one of those shortcuts is probably not worth the pain the next day from management. Whilst

I've never been uploaded to a website, I've taken a shortcut once or twice on a delivery, though I'd like to think my assumption was correct, that the customer was in fact not home.

Take, for example, this:

A postie becomes familiar with delivering to certain streets and neighbourhoods over the course of time, gets to know the customers personally, and gains knowledge of what vehicles are parked at certain residences at various times of the day. Sometimes a postie may even have a conversation with a customer who might tell them their work hours, so the postie develops an understanding of who's home and who's at work on any given day of the week.

Complacency, however, has been known to set in as a delivery officer. A customer might have dropped their car to a mechanic for the day and been given a lift back home.

You see where I'm going with this?

Assuming that a customer isn't home just because their car isn't in the driveway doesn't always mean they aren't home. Avoiding the walk to the front door to save 30 seconds may just be the dumbest thing a postie could do, because apart from the obvious, Karen may be filming their *lack of judgement*.

Personally, I don't condone the idea of taking a shortcut when it comes to customer service (though, as already explained, I've done it once or twice). Still, it baffles me as to why a more up-front approach isn't taken by the customer themselves. Maybe it's my old-school upbringing, but I was always told to be up-front with someone if they upset me rather than let it stew for too long.

In the case of uploading videos of people making errors in judgement, well, that's really letting it stew well past the maximum cooking time, in my humble opinion once again. If I could offer some advice on both examples, it would be this:

Never assume, as a delivery officer, that no one's home, even if the driveway's empty, the blinds are down, and the place has about as much life to it as a morgue. If you have Karen-like tendencies and spot a postie out the front writing out a card, why not try a simple:

"YOOHOO, POSTIE! I'M HOME!!"

Rather than sharing a video on social media platforms for the world to see?

It's how friendships are formed, just ask Mrs Smith.

'Foot In Mouth Disease'

One thing I've been guilty of in the past is a regular case of foot-in-mouth disease that's seen me back-pedalling like Michael Jackson's famous moonwalk. Let's face it, being a postie presents regular contact with customers, and personally, I've found that the 'straight-up' approach is usually well received.

"G'day Mrs Smith, how's those West Coast Eagles of yours on the weekend, ey?"

Or:

"Got a parcel for you, Jack. How's things going, and is there a silly chance your Fremantle Dockers could actually go all the way this year?"

You know, basic banter.

Trying to pre-empt, however, what may be going on in a customer's household at any time can be fraught with danger, hence my next story:

I had been delivering to an elderly couple for many years and had got to know them well. They used to bring me a drink on arrival at their house on a warm day, and I'd throw a tennis ball to their dog on many occasions while talking about the weather, AFL, and whatever else came to mind on days when a chat with their postie seemed to bring a smile to the faces of 'Hazel' and 'Bob'.

When I returned from holidays one year, I sorted a registered letter from a local funeral home addressed to Hazel, which I initially thought was rather unusual. Hazel and Bob were as fit as fiddles, perhaps early 70s, always happy, smiling, running around after their beloved dog and, in general, an absolute joy to have as customers on my delivery round. So, a letter from a funeral home to this postie spelt one thing and one thing only:

They were paying their bill in advance, no risk at all. (I believe you can do that nowadays.) Great assumption, GT.

"Hi Hazel, haven't seen you for a couple of weeks, been on holidays, however I have a letter for you from the local funeral home. You aren't planning on going anywhere anytime soon, are you??!!"

"Oh dear, didn't you hear? Bob passed away, complications in surgery. It was so sudden."

I immediately wished for the ground to swallow me up and make me disappear, though Hazel wouldn't have any of my apology. In fact, she told me that she and Bob used to love my straight-up approach and looked forward to some regular banter with their postie.

From that day on, however, I just tweaked that straight-up approach ever so slightly.

It always pays to let the customer TELL YOU what's going on in their household rather than the other way around. Many factors to the job of delivery, many situations that are usually filled with a smile or a laugh, and then there's the occasional situation where you wish you had simply toned down the initial greeting.

We live and we learn.

'Not recognising your Postie'

I've often wondered why some people I've delivered to in suburbia have ignored me the very next day when I've spotted them in a supermarket, despite no real difference in the way I looked outside of work hours.

I used to always wear a baseball cap while delivering parcels to an area I serviced for around five or so years on the south coast, and the only thing missing from my Saturday morning shopping attire compared to a weekday delivering parcels was the colour of my shirt, as I dressed rather simply, to say the least. (Wal told me a rather funny story a while ago about a fellow employee who used to wear his postie uniform on the weekend when he went shopping!)

I suppose my dress sense wasn't far off that example, minus the work shirt, of course.

Weekdays: a yellow postie shirt, black or blue shorts, black baseball cap, Nike tennis shoes.

Saturday morning supermarket shop: a different coloured shirt, black or blue shorts, same black baseball cap, same Nike shoes, same silly grin.

I've had some customers tell me the equivalent of their life story on a doorstep some days, including the details of their marriage breakup, what university their kids were studying at, what they were going to be doing on the weekend, plus what alcohol, and how much of it, they'd be consuming that same afternoon. Yet, they ignored me the very next day outside of work, and I found it fascinating, to say the least.

Some customers spill their hearts out to someone they barely know but trust all the same, as they get some things off their chest that may have been bothering them, or perhaps they're just a bit lonely and in need of a chat. Either way, I was always happy to lend an ear.

At times, I'd catch a regular customer's eye at a food store and say something like, "Hi there, it's your postie, sorry I don't have my uniform on or my bike helmet, but it's me all the same. How are you?" (Why would I say sorry?! Yet I did sometimes, as if I'd let them down by actually having a life outside of being a postie!)

Remember Superman? Even Clark Kent had a life outside of the red cape.

Personally, I used to love a chat with a customer on a doorstep, but it was also a nice vibe to see that same customer in the main street outside of work and be recognised as more than just the person who delivered their bills or parcels. I once had someone say to me, "Oh, you look different without your helmet on."

Same face, same silly grin, just a different hat. When Clark Kent put his glasses on, c'mon, he still looked like Superman didn't he?!

The 'Talkative' Customer

(Playing tennis)

I like to talk; I have no qualms whatsoever in admitting that, and perhaps it's why I like to write, it's a form of getting things off one's chest. When having a conversation with a customer though, I generally like it to be how a game of tennis should be played, and that generally equates to an average-paced rally that may last a couple of minutes or so, as a bit of a guide, anyhow.

If ever I was involved in a long rally on a tennis court, I'd usually look at somehow ending the rally eventually because of the obvious, there's more to life than simply knocking a ball over a net. And as enjoyable as it can be, it can also be rather tiresome.

So, when having a conversation with someone at their front doorstep, the 'rally' usually needed to be kept to a minimum of, say, 40 shots, and the pace required consistency: back and forth without one player dominating the pace too much.

Sometimes it could be a little unsettling when the 'opponent' dictated the rally and their pace was pushing me back to the baseline further and further until I was more or less making my way through the gate and back to my vehicle.

You still with me, or have I lost you on this one?

There have been some deliveries where the rally (conversation) commenced at the doorstep and only ended when I decided that my safest option was to get into the van or onto my bike and get out of there as quickly, and as politely, as I could, of course.

If you're a customer who likes to 'play tennis' (talk) with your postie, and perhaps someone who loves a long rally, try to finish the point within a respectable timeframe, please, as the postie has the equivalent of five sets of tennis to play on most days of deliveries.

In saying that, thank you sincerely for being a talkative and friendly customer, as it's a whole lot more fun delivering to people like you than delivering to 'Bernie'.

Chapter 3:
The Postie, Way Too Much Fun,
Dog Stories, A Day In The Life

The Postie

Before the internet became such an integral part of everyone's lives and online shopping commenced, the postie was basically the *bill delivery person* and relied on to deliver water, gas, electricity, rates, and phone bills.

(Yep, the bearer of bad news, basically.)

I vividly recall some days where Synergy, Telstra or Western Power utility bills arrived on the same day as the local rates, and that meant just about every single house required a delivery. However, that wasn't really the difficult part of it all, it was the sorting.

Some days it would take almost six hours of sorting to deliver for about three hours on the road, and by the end of the initial sorting, the brain would be completely frazzled, for want of a better word. I've mentioned it later in this book, however it's probably worth repeating that a day like the one above could just be nudging the 3,000-letter/oversized-article volume type of day, perhaps more.

Take, for example, a delivery round of approximately 1,000 letterboxes where almost every single delivery point had two utility bills. Then there'd be a generous portion of addresses that received a personal letter (because that's how people communicated back in the day) and perhaps an oversized article such as an A4 document or a magazine.

A big business, however, may have had 20 items alone, so the figure of 3,000 items that required sorting by a postie on a busy morning may just be fairly close to the mark. Of course, we're going back in time, like Dr Who in his Tardis, to almost black-and-white television days when life was a lot simpler. It was also well before customers received their utility bills online and when people communicated with ink on paper.

Those huge mail-volume days required some seriously fancy sorting by a postie to make the 5 pm delivery deadline.

If an address didn't have a letterbox at the time of delivery (some fell apart, some got stolen, and some premises didn't actually own a letterbox at all), it was up to the discretion of the postie what to do with the letter. Personally, unless the property housed an aggressive dog, I'd wedge the letter in the front door or under the door, or simply place it on the front door mat.

The other option was to return the letter to the sender by way of a stamp that stated *'No Letterbox'.*

Personally, I preferred to not do this as I did not wish to be held responsible for a customer calling Synergy with the old line "I didn't even receive my first bill so why are you sending me another one?"

(Follow-up invoices were commonplace and sent out if they were not paid within a 'reasonable' time frame.)

I'll never forget, possibly in just my second week on the job, delivering an item to a customer who told me that I was her "most favourite person in the world" (and I don't believe at the time it had anything to do with my looks). I don't recall what I delivered to her, but at a guess, perhaps a passport, because back when I started, we didn't deliver online shopping items because obviously, online shopping didn't exist.

To be honest, a passport was really the only exciting thing we delivered apart from Christmas and birthday cards.

I remember vividly, on my way home that day, thinking about that comment and how many other jobs I'd done in my life that basically offered no positive feedback, only something negative if you stuffed something up.

The social interaction of a delivery should never be taken for granted and personally, I never took it for granted (unless the customer was a pain in the arse), particularly if you're a bit of a chatterbox like me and don't mind a bit of banter.

Some quiet days on the job blew out to some rather modest finishing times due to the number of customers who may have required some assistance with something, or perhaps a chat, which may have cost me five or ten minutes of delivery time here and there.

There are probably not too many posties out there (particularly those who have spent quite a few years in the system) who haven't rendered some form of assistance to a customer or three over their career, whether it was verbally or physically.

By that, I refer to something as simple as helping an elderly customer who may have just returned from their grocery shopping and needed a helping hand taking some bags inside, or someone who just wanted to talk footy, AFL or otherwise. I once pushed a vehicle for a bloke who was trying to jump-start his car on his own, and after we got him going, he did a quick trip around the block to thank me before going on his merry way.

I was only a postie, but I was relied on by many customers to help them get through their day for reasons that had nothing to do with delivering parcels or utility bills, and a conversation could make someone's day, particularly if they lived alone. The number of things that could happen in suburbia on any given day are obviously endless, and a postie could often be caught in the firing line.

Personally, I managed to complete the quartet of the Australian Postal Industry, which first began on a pushbike before upgrading to a motorbike round, which then led to a walk delivery round incorporating a business district, and then the final piece of my delivery jigsaw was completed with van deliveries.

I avoided the current era of the three-wheeler or 'EV' (Electric Vehicle), just like several of my former workmates have, though we often dissect the new system of delivery over an ale or two and talk about the what-ifs, and how we'd all perhaps handle, or not handle, the new technology.

If ever I make a comeback of sorts (which I doubt), I promise you I'll rewrite this book and include a few three-wheeler or EV stories.

Way Too Much Fun

Looking back, my previous years of employment lacked any type of future, and I had finally been presented with something that I believed had substance, something that I liked the idea of from that very first day.

Most jobs I'd tried previously had an aura about them that only spelled one word: *work.*

The thing that struck me most about the Honda 110 was the fact that it was the type of bike a kid could ride, someone who'd only just hung up their trainer wheels and was looking for some quicker transport, yet here I was, riding one and getting paid a fortnightly wage for the privilege.

The 110 was an easy bike to ride as it had an automatic clutch, or as I was told by my riding instructor, a 'centrifugal clutch', terminology that flew straight over my head like a pigeon in full flight. I just nodded and smiled as if I knew what he was talking about.

The Honda would save my legs, and my dwindling weight, for that matter, as I'd lost 7 kg in my first two months on the job, pushing a heavy bag of mail around on the front of a pushbike that had just one gear. No amount of food would replenish my system after four hours of mail delivery, sometimes more, though I gave it a fair nudge most afternoons once I'd finished my round.

Before I upgraded to the Honda, I'd dropped to 64 kg in eight weeks of pedalling. For a bloke of almost six foot, that's fairly light-on. I'd started the job at around 71 kg, give or take a donut or two.

So, back to mail delivery, it wasn't hard. In fact, it was outrageously enjoyable, perhaps even way too much fun.

I mean, here I was sitting on a motorbike, sliding letters and magazines into letterboxes, and getting paid good money to do so. When I say *good money*, well, it was for me, as I had no trade and no real desire to do much, to be perfectly honest. I just drifted from one job to another, earning enough to afford the rent, food, and a few beers each week.

Mail delivery in suburbia, however, was a whole new kettle of fish, and right from day one on the job, I could see a future in it. I had finally found something that would not only give me some excess money after rent, food, and beer, but it would also give me a feeling of accomplishment. Not many jobs do that, trust me, I've tried a few.

Chasing Dogs

Why am I doing this?

I can't drive…

(Jimeoin, comical genius, and his take on what dogs perhaps think when they sit back and ponder why on earth they are bothering with the whole tiresome process of chasing vehicles.)

There was one element of the job I was told about on day one at Postie School that was, and possibly still is, regarded as the most dangerous:

The dog.

Forget distracted or careless motorists who didn't see the bike, or uncomfortable wet-weather days; the dog could be the most frightening part of being a postie. The thought of losing a limb, or at least part of one, could send even the bravest delivery officers into panic mode.

Being a new postie, however, can bring a sense of bravado, lack of fear, lack of common sense, or all of the above. Looking back, I suppose I had all those traits, as I was simply trying to make an impression, one way or another.

No dog was going to ruin my bright new start in life. I believe it was probably only about a month or so after I had upgraded to the Honda that I decided to do a bit of chasing myself, just on the spur of the moment.

I'm not sure why I even attempted the reverse chase, but I'm glad I did. It proved one thing: a dog is not always the bully they make themselves out to be when the roles are reversed. I had heard about the old postie/dog thing since I was a kid and had witnessed it several times, but when I was thrust into the same situation, I felt a strange sense of authority and lack of fear.

Initially, the dog chased me, but dogs get tired, and eventually they run out of puff. That's when I decided to get my own back and chase him. As I distanced myself from him at the start of his pursuit, I had another bright spark moment and thought to myself: *I wonder what would happen if...*

And so, I did.

I chased that particular dog for approximately 200 metres on the Honda (and may have offered some words of advice as well) before heading back to the area where he had initially started chasing me. I finished the mail delivery for that street with a smile and a sense of pride I had never felt before in a workplace.

I was now a postie, an integral part of the streets of suburbia; an 'eyes on the street' type of public figure, someone to bring joy to customers at Christmas or on birthdays with cards, a person who makes life seem okay simply by being there each day.

Cooper, The Rottweiler

I had been servicing an area for several years on the south coast of WA, and one dog who left an impression on me was an absolute basket case, he went nuts every time he saw me pull up on the bike.

His name was Cooper, a Rottweiler.

My most vivid memory of Cooper was him on a leash pegged to a stake in the ground. On seeing me ride up, he ripped the peg out just as I neared the letterbox and chased me down the road. They didn't get their mail that day.

Each Christmas, the owners felt sorry for me and would leave a six-pack of beer for putting up with their animal who despised me. I kid you not, they always bought Coopers brewed beer. Their sense of humour was brilliant.

Some days, I would ride past him and his owner as they walked the neighbourhood. It was like watching a scene from a comedy movie, with the owner leaning back almost horizontally to hold the animal on the leash as it tried to attack me.

I'm not sure why he wanted to bite me; all I ever did was deliver their mail and parcels, and I reckon I did a fair job most days. Whenever I spotted Cooper outside (usually to the left of their property in a designated area), I would ride past the house, park the bike, then sneak up to either the letterbox or front porch, out of the dog's view, and deliver the goods, just praying he wouldn't catch my scent.

The very next postie who took over from me was, by chance, related to Cooper's owners. I think it was only a matter of weeks before he got bitten, and Cooper did serious damage to his leg. The poor bugger had to go to hospital to get a nasty wound stitched and had about two weeks off work.

I look back on that situation with mixed emotions and often wondered if it was my fault for not warning the new postie. I must admit, though, I was thankful to have avoided Cooper's grasp, he had bloody big teeth.

Since the new postie was related to the owners, I didn't think I needed to warn him, surely he knew Cooper was a bit of a livewire. I take no responsibility for that one. I just hope they left him at least a carton of Coopers ale the next Christmas, as he definitely deserved more than a six-pack.

Macca, The Dog Whisperer

I was taught by Macca on the south coast to offer dogs a treat and not be scared of them, get them on your side; reverse psychology of sorts. If you took a packet of treats with you and gave one to a dog, it would often change their behaviour when they heard the bike.

The problem was obvious: it was the noise of the bike that drove a dog crazy.

I was once shown by a workmate that switching the bike off could actually settle a dog, sometimes to the point where it totally lost interest and simply walked off. I tried it, some dogs did lose interest, while others still tried to jump the fence to get to me. Whether it works or not is still up for debate.

However, with a treat as an incentive to be friendly, most dogs looked forward to seeing the postie instead of trying to bite them. I can honestly say it worked almost every time. I used to buy a packet each fortnight, around $4 worth, cheap, considering it may keep a dog happy and a postie safe.

(I still believe a packet of dog treats should be claimed as a tax deduction, part of a postie's survival kit.)

Macca was a genius, a dog whisperer of sorts. He would leave notes for me if I was delivering some of his mail while he was away, or if I was helping him on a busy day and he wanted one of his dogs fed.

A typical note from Macca might read:

"Go to side gate, take 2 biscuits, throw one to Buster, then give another to Billy as he's old and will just sit there."

Macca also stated:

"Remember GT, always ask a customer if you see them outside whether it's okay to feed their dog or dogs. Most say it's fine as they understand it may help with postie/dog relations, but there could be a downside to the idea."

"If someone sees a postie hand a treat to a dog and then enter their premises, well, it might be an easy way for someone to find themselves a new television too."

"You with me?"

I understood what he was saying; Macca was all over this concept like a seagull onto a chip.

Macca knew everything about every dog in every neighbourhood, and he treated them all as if he owned them himself. He once told me about a big dog he trained to grab the mail from him with its teeth and run it back to its owner. This little circus act was apparently going beautifully, until Macca went on holidays and didn't tell the relief postie about their routine.

By all reports, the new postie could be heard yelling out the front at the letterbox as the big fella bailed him up, wishing for nothing but the mail. But hey, the new postie didn't know that, now did he?!

It always pays to tell the new postie if you have a system like that; it can save a bit of stress. I knew there was more to the whole postie/dog relationship than my early days in the job, when I basically feared for my life at some addresses.

Get to know your customer, human or otherwise. Pretty simple, really.

A Day in the Life (Sporting Legends)

To those who have never worked in the industry (and this is just my take), the one thing to remember when working as a postie is that no two days are the same, and I believe that's the overriding factor that makes the job so enjoyable.

Let's face it, once your mail, parcels, or both are packed and ready to go, the world is your oyster. Out in suburbia, anything can happen, and you can meet some pretty interesting people, and perhaps the occasional sporting legend.

My hero as a kid was none other than the great Dennis Lillee, a sporting rock star of sorts, larger than life and someone any budding young cricketer would want to emulate.

The thought of meeting the man personally responsible for making cricket huge in the 70's and early 80's, and who inspired me to play the sport, was ridiculously appealing. I was told early on by a few fellow posties that Dennis was a local.

'Burnsey' (who I have written fondly about in this book) once told me that while he was at a fuel station filling up his bike one morning, the great man walked past him. Out of respect, Burnsey called out, "Morning, Mr Lillee!"

Dennis's reply?

"Morning mate, but please call me Dennis, Mr Lillee is my dad." Classic.

I did in fact meet Dennis when I was assigned to the delivery round where he lived, and he had to be one of the nicest blokes I had ever met. At the time, he was still rolling the arm over at Lilac Hill each year, minus the long flowing locks, and a little less pace, yet the action remained. Oh, that action, poetry.

He had made the front cover of the *West Australian* newspaper in that iconic pose, almost pleading with the umpire for LBW. The picture had to be signed; I wasn't letting that one pass. I bought a copy and left it in the back parcel container on my bike, hoping I'd get a chance to ask him to sign it, and he did later that same week.

Legend, DK.

Just as a bit of added nostalgia: Dad took my cricket bat when I was about eight to get signed by Dennis when he visited my hometown of Albany, WA in the late 70's. Dad always used to say about meeting a celebrity:

"They've only got two arms and two legs, Glenn, just like you."

It was his way of telling me never to shy away from saying g'day or having a chat with someone legendary, embrace the situation, which of course I did with Dennis. Twenty-odd years later, the great man added his signature to some more DK memorabilia for a die-hard fan.

I also had the pleasure of both meeting and delivering mail to legendary three-time AFL premiership coach Mick Malthouse, who isn't as grumpy as the media used to portray him. Personally, I think he simply despised giving press conferences, but I always found him polite whenever I saw him in his front yard on mail deliveries.

Baseball Bats (no questions asked)

On van deliveries several years back, I delivered a baseball bat to an address I considered somewhat on the 'dodgy' side. I didn't hand it to the customer, though, I handed it to a police officer. There were three or four police cars parked out the front that morning, and it wasn't the first time I'd seen them there.

I took the bat out of the back of the van and approached two officers.

"Morning, gentlemen. Obviously, a bit going on here, but any chance you could please give this to the tenant?"

The bat was a safe-drop item, so no signature was required; it just had to be scanned and left in a safe place. The officer I handed it to laughed and said, "Yeah, no problem. We'll make sure he gets it."

I often wondered what the customer had planned for the bat, it wasn't something I regularly delivered. But as the saying goes: *not ours to know the reason why.* That sums up the postie gig: just deliver it, don't ask questions.

Wayward Wildlife

Delivering a cat to a vet clinic ranks as one of the more unique things I've delivered, despite an unfortunate ending.

I found the cat sleeping on a verge next to a busy road. Others might have assumed it was deceased, but to me it looked like it was just sleeping, unusual given the location. On picking him up, I could tell he needed help, so I placed him in the front mail carrier on the Honda and headed to the nearest vet clinic.

The vet told me she'd look him over and I left my number. She rang later that day to tell me they had unfortunately had to put him down due to head trauma, likely from being hit by a car, which explained why he was sleeping near the main road.

At least he got a dignified send-off, and I'm glad I picked him up and got him out of harm's way.

Another wildlife story worth mentioning involved a wayward family of ducks. A mother duck and her ducklings had taken a wrong turn one morning, and I spotted them trying to navigate a busy intersection on a highway. A few cars had stopped for them, and that's when I had another rare moment of excellence, something that never happened at school, unfortunately.

I told a lady in the first vehicle that I would see if I could convince them to go the right way. I knew exactly where they needed to go, a pond about 100 metres away, as I was familiar with the area.

So away we went.

Mother duck and her ducklings started heading towards the pond as I manoeuvred the Honda behind them. The rest was easy, I simply followed them on the footpath all the way back. It was one of the most unique starts to a day of delivering mail I'd ever experienced.

The 'Spider in the Letterbox' Customer

I used to deliver to an address on the south coast of WA that owned a 'pet' huntsman spider. Now, when I say 'pet', I mean it like this: the people who lived there treated it like their pet because it was a small letterbox, and it was rather obvious the big, furry fella had set up camp. They obviously didn't mind him living there.

Personally, I hate spiders, particularly huntsman spiders. They have a bit of a presence with those long, hairy legs, and if you've ever had the 'pleasure' of finding one behind your sun visor, you'll know they can literally scare the crap out of you.

Back to the letterbox in question: after a while, I sort of got used to him being there. If I had to open the letterbox to place an item in, I did it carefully. Most of the time, I'd avoid opening it altogether and simply place items in the top area of the letterbox, which had a V-shaped compartment.

If you fit the description of owning a 'pet' spider in your letterbox, perhaps leave a small note for the postie or junk mail delivery person to look out for it. Scaring the postie isn't cool and probably isn't mentioned in any manual on 'How to be a Successful Postie,' so please, don't invent ways to make a postie's job harder.

Online shopping makes the job complicated enough as it is.

Chapter 4:
Sorry We Missed You,
The Letterbox, Lawn Etiquette

'Sorry We Missed You'

I touched on this with the 'deaf customer', but there are several layers to the situation, and I'll do my best to explain them.

As explained earlier, it's not always the postie's fault if a customer finds a card wedged in their door or letterbox stating, *'Sorry We Missed You'*, even though they were home at the time.

A card should only ever be left in a letterbox if it's not possible to get to the front door safely. A card wedged in a front door shows the postie made an effort, whereas a letterbox card doesn't really give off that impression. I learned that the hard way one day and had a tough time explaining it to management.

After knocking on the front door and receiving no answer, I realized I had no cards on me; usually, I kept half a dozen in my pocket. I walked back down the stairs to the van, grabbed a card, wrote out the details of the item, and then did something I regret: I put the card in the letterbox to save the walk back up the steps. Dumb idea.

The chances of the whole scenario playing out like this were rather slim, yet it happened; after returning to the office, the boss quizzed me about the card in the letterbox because you guessed it, the customer was in fact home, found the card in the letterbox then rang through a complaint and that of course was; "The postie didn't knock on my door, left a card in my letterbox, obviously couldn't be bothered to see if we were home".

After explaining the situation, which I'm not sure he believed, I told myself from that day onwards to always make the trek back to the front door to wedge the card in, if I ever ran out in my pocket, just to show I had made the effort of knocking. You with me?

Only signature items require the customer to be home at the time of delivery. There's no excuse not to leave a safe-drop item unless there are security concerns, for example, a resident dog discovering and eating it. A postie needs to weigh up each delivery situation because some can go pear-shaped, even if they seem straightforward at the time.

I've seen hilarious skits on social media portraying the postie tip-toeing up to a front door, knocking no louder than a mouse would with a sturdy fist, leaving a card for collection at the local postal outlet, then sprinting back to the vehicle. Exaggerated, perhaps, but very amusing. Some customers swear the scenario is real.

The person who copped the abuse from the customer was rarely the postie; it was the unsuspecting Oz Post employee at the pick-up location who had to relay the message that usually went something like this:

"Here's my card and can you please tell the useless f'n postie that I was home thanks?"

"Sure, I'll pass it on. Sorry."

I've been in that situation myself on the south coast, filling in as the 'hatch guy' who answers the bell, takes the card (and abuse), then locates the item. Yep, a character builder.

I reiterate: there are many reasons a postie knocking on a door may go unheard, and it's not just because someone might be hard of hearing. I've had to weigh up countless situations as a postie, but delivering an item is always easier and less complicated than carding one. I've always done my best to offload an item rather than take it back to the office.

Any delivery person who takes pleasure in sorting dozens or hundreds of items, loading a vehicle, arriving at an address, and then reversing the process without trying everything to deliver the item should, in my humble opinion, be locked up in the nearest mental asylum.

On more than one occasion, I have knocked on a customer's front door, received no reply, yet heard voices from inside the house, which, on closer inspection, I found were coming from the back yard. So, I gave up knocking on the front door and yelled over the back fence that the postie had arrived. The item was delivered, and the customer appreciated the effort. Seriously, what's quicker, a brisk walk around the back, or the long, drawn-out process of writing out a card and rescanning the item?

A pet dog has also prevented deliveries on more than one occasion. Most dog owners let you know whether it's safe to go through the front gate, but when a postie first starts a round, it's up to them to assess the risk.

Look, I wasn't stupid in my delivery days. If bailed up by a foot-long lapdog, I took my chances. But deciding whether to open the gate to a Rottweiler or German Shepherd was never a hard decision.

Another common situation I encountered was the 'Fort Knox' style property where some customers like to hide away, which makes deliveries rather difficult. I've seen all sorts of front walls and gate designs that leave the postie guessing what's on the other side. Some addresses resemble a compound, those deliveries are always challenging.

If an address had no buzzer and I couldn't see what was inside the property, I would card the item. Personally, I needed to know what was inside the fence, rather than guess, as that's how a postie could lose a limb to a guard dog.

The only other reason a postie may card an item is if they simply don't like you personally, which I highly doubt. I have delivered to old girlfriends and blokes that I may have had a dust-up with at a local pub when we were lads, where carding the item may have been safer, but I simply left the sunnies on, knocked on the door and hoped they didn't recognise me.

So there you have it: the most common reasons a postie might write a card stating *'Sorry We Missed You'*. I hope it brings some closure on a bone-of-contention in the postal industry.

The Letterbox

The letterbox is the final piece of the daily jigsaw puzzle for a postie when it comes to mail sorting and delivery. If you don't get that last piece completed with a minimum of fuss, it can make the day feel long.

Every postie has had a moment with a letterbox that seemed to need a good talking-to, as though it were a person misbehaving. I'm sure most posties have had one of *those* moments where abusing a letterbox might have been overheard by Mrs Smith in her front yard, pruning behind a rose bush.

"YA F...N USELESS F...N THING!"

(It's then you realise someone's within earshot of your verbal tirade.)

"Oh Mrs Smith, didn't see you there! Just singing a bit of rap out loud, apologies..."

That happened to me on more than one occasion, though my excuses varied depending on the customer's initial reaction to my 'singing.'

After a bit of rain, it can be a real character builder finding room in a letterbox slot next to junk mail or a newspaper delivered earlier that morning or the previous afternoon.

Junk mail and newspaper services aren't silly; they know when the main postal service rolls out and usually when it's finished, so they step in to deliver their own pamphlets and papers. All part of the fun.

The most frustrating part about rival deliveries is when the slot reserved for a newspaper or bulkier junk mail is ignored, and they stuff their product into the mail slot. On a wet day, that can drive a postie nuts, paper expands when wet, making some slots almost impossible to use.

The best letterboxes I've delivered to are ones that can take an A-4 sized envelope or magazine with a lift-up lid so no matter what you have for a customer, it fits. One of the worst I have delivered to is the type from the days of black-and-white TV, made from concrete or bricks and only wide and deep enough to take around 3 or 4 letters. Any oversized items are basically impossible to squeeze in.

Not sure what they were thinking back then, but the slots were clearly measured to the exact width of a letter, with no thought that one day letters might grow in size or that magazines and larger items might need to be delivered.

Without a doubt, though, the all-time worst letterbox I've delivered to (and I'm certain more than one postie will back me up) is the *hollow log on a stand* style. The maker of this one should be fined for mail abuse: the slot takes no more than two or three letters deep and isn't wide enough for the width of a standard letter. How did this even get through the system?

I haven't seen any newer versions, so hopefully it was a one-off. If you own one, can I suggest replacing it eventually? I'm only thinking of the well-being of your items.

One letterbox that still baffles me isn't the box itself, but how it's mounted. It's a basic 3- to 4-foot-high flip-lid letterbox that should have the slot at the front, yet about a third of them are installed back to front.

True story.

C'mon, when you bought that letterbox, you had one job. You're better than that, fix it.

I've seen letterboxes so stuffed with junk mail, newspapers, and mail from a week earlier that I haven't even tried front entry; all that does is clutter it up more. When confronted with that scenario, it's easier on both the patience and the body to lean around the back and attempt rear entry, so to speak.

I know some of these postie terms are difficult to follow if you haven't been in the system, and I apologise if they sound a little rude or unflattering.

I once delivered to an address with an old microwave oven mounted on a pole as a letterbox. Ingenious, plenty of room for any article, and it still opened with the same button as though it were plugged in and operating. That's unique.

Kurt, another postie I've written fondly about in this book, once told me he fell off his pushbike when his ring finger got stuck in a letterbox. The metal opening at the front caught his finger. I've delivered to these designs regularly, and I concur with Kurt, they have a spring, not unlike a mousetrap. Not sure why they were made this way; the springs in some are a little on the 'non-postie-user-friendly' side.

In the good old days, it was normal to deliver mail while riding along, without stopping, just a slight break in pace as you approached a letterbox, with mail ready in your left hand if on a motorbike, or right hand if on a pushbike.

It was commonly known as 'on-the-fly.'

That was the quickest way of doing things, and it wasn't unusual to deliver an entire street without coming to a complete stop. At the end of a run like that, you were looking for a bit of crowd interaction; a fist pump in the air wasn't uncommon.

Here's a true story:

On-the-fly delivery became such an integral part of my daily routine on the bike that one day after work, I was posting a personal letter into a red street mailbox and as I walked towards it, I flicked it in without breaking stride, as if I were still on bike delivery. Some habits are tough to break.

Back in the day, to deliver an entire street on-the-fly, the letterboxes had to be of good quality. On some streets, you could almost set your stopwatch; on others, you just knew it was going to be a long, drawn-out process. Some houses still have a slot in the front door from the days of posties on foot, and some posties still deliver to it rather than ask a 100-year-old customer to "please get with the program."

Seriously though, customers, think of your postie: they have up to 1,500 delivery points to get through each day, so a bit of consideration wouldn't go astray when it comes to letterbox placement and slot size.

Some customers receive truckloads of mail yet own something that resembles a shoebox fit only for a mouse. The postie then has to either bend the mail and magazines out of shape to make them fit, or get off the bike and leave them on the front doorstep.

Some letterboxes are placed in really strange spots, as if to tease the postie. I've seen one at the top of a driveway so steep it was too dangerous to tackle on the way up. Stalling a postie bike is common, but on that particular delivery point, it could have ended badly if the bike had decided to have a nap, as they do from time to time.

Instead, I had to go full throttle to the top of the driveway with the mail ready in my right hand (even though that's the throttle side of the bike), do a loop at the top, then ease the mail into the letterbox while slowly rolling back down with my foot firmly on the brake.

There's an art to delivering to crappy letterboxes, particularly those in awkward locations. I'm a firm believer in using common sense. On that hilltop letterbox, I simply started leaving the customer's mail on the doorstep after the first day rather than repeat the tedious routine I've just described, and I never once received a complaint.

Maybe that's why they built it where they did: to get the mail delivered straight to the doorstep. I used to come up with a term for certain letterboxes I believed were built or placed just to annoy the postie: I called them 'cut lunch and a water bag' letterboxes. I'm sure you can work that one out.

If you own one, please make an adjustment for the postie's sake, trust me, they'll appreciate it, and you won't hear the occasional verbal barrage aimed at it on delivery.

No one really knows why a customer would place a letterbox in the middle of their lawn, then call to complain that the postie left tyre marks on it. Believe me, it's true, it's happened to me and several other posties I know.

The only way to avoid a situation like that is for the delivery officer to consider all possible angles of delivery and vary the approach each day, which may give the lawn a bit of relief. Probably easier to move the letterbox to the side of the driveway, but that might make too much sense.

Some letterboxes need to be reconstructed after every delivery because they fall apart regularly. The postie finds this out when trying to put something larger than a letter in, only for the whole thing to collapse. The next day, it's usually back up and running.

Every postie has a story about a letterbox that has given them sleepless nights, wondering how they'll tackle the beast the next day.

Lawn Etiquette

Lawn and letterboxes go hand in hand as they're part of the same process, the final part of delivery. So why is it such an issue at times?

Simple answer is this: the customer would like their lawn to remain relatively untouched by the wheels of the delivery vehicle; however, the location of their letterbox is perhaps too close to the lawn, hence the postie having to 'borrow' a bit of lawn to complete a delivery.

Then the issue begins with a phone call to management stating, "The postie is continually riding over my lawn and leaving a mark." (Not sure how many times I've seen or heard that complaint come through over the years.)

OK, let's look at it in detail:

If the letterbox is nowhere near the front lawn, then basically the postie shouldn't be riding over the lawn. However, there may be some extenuating factors that could let the postie off the hook regarding a lawn ride-over, so to speak. If a car is parked too close to the letterbox, then a postie may have to borrow that bit of lawn I mentioned earlier, without taking the piss.

In other words, a postie may need to ride over a small section of grass to get close enough to the letterbox to deliver the goods, but without going straight across the fully manicured 'bowling green' lawn that some 'curators' spend hours on each week, just to get it looking pristine and the envy of the neighbours.

So, a little leniency may have to be shown in certain delivery situations.

I know what you're thinking: Why doesn't the useless f'n postie just get off their bike and walk to the letterbox??!!

The answer is simple:

Because if every delivery point on a round of approximately 1,500 letterboxes required parking the bike (which would obviously force the postie to walk to the letterbox), it may as well become a 'walk round' as opposed to a bike round. Plus, it would send the required delivery time for that round into a new stratosphere.

You with me? It's a time factor.

Another factor regarding the lawn is that it may not actually be the postie causing the damage, as there are numerous other delivery organisations out there trying to get their product delivered daily. So, if you have a rogue delivery person ruining your lawn without justification, then I suggest you either take a photo of them in action or grab the number plate of the offending vehicle.

Oz Post employees have a fairly distinctive uniform, so unless it looks rather obvious which organisation is doing the deliveries, then I'd suggest it's not Oz Post but a junk mail delivery service.

At Postie School, etiquette *is* taught, trust me on this one, but that's not to say some may not own as much etiquette as others, same as in all walks of life.

In conclusion: if your letterbox is set up in a way that allows the postie to do their job with minimum fuss (and minimum lawn borrowing), then I think you and your postie will get along famously, with no need whatsoever to ring through a complaint stating your delivery person is an absolute nob who needs to lift their game.

The postie/customer relationship is real; it's like the postie/dog interaction. On most occasions, it's harmony, but every now and then, it all goes pear-shaped. Fact of life.

The 'Duck Down and Hide' Customer

I've had the following situation occur during motorcycle deliveries on a couple of occasions, and it's usually when a registered letter from a legal firm is sent out, often a demand for legal fees or perhaps a summons to court to pay those fees. It can be rather uncomfortable for not only the customer but also the postie who is just trying to do their job.

I vividly recall one of those encounters. I parked the bike and went in search of a customer's signature for a registered letter; the front door was ajar, and a flyscreen door secured the premises. Obviously, I couldn't knock on the flyscreen, so I offered a verbal greeting: "Hi, anyone home? It's the postie!"

As I glanced through the flyscreen door, I saw someone duck below the kitchen bench.

On further inspection, I noticed that the registered letter I had for the customer was from a lawyer's office. (The customer obviously knew it was probably on its way.) So, I repeated the greeting.

Nothing.

I felt like saying, "C'mon, I know you're in there," yet that's not part of a postie's job description, so I simply wrote out a card for them and placed it under the door. I'm uncertain whether the recipient contacted the lawyer's office or not, but I played my part as the delivery guy, and that's where my responsibility ended.

I suppose if nothing else, it may have bought the customer a bit more time to save up for the legal fees.

One of my fellow workmates did take issue with this type of customer and did, in fact, say what I wasn't prepared to say, and that didn't go down too well. From memory, a complaint was sent through to Oz Post stating they didn't appreciate the postie's refusal to accept that they 'weren't home', even though my workmate swore they were home as he spotted the customer ducking for cover.

Is it just me, or is there a bit of irony in that complaint?

Chapter 5:
Early Days, Kenny and Leapy

The highlight of my working life, without a doubt, was securing a position as a postie at 'The Post Office' in a northern suburb of Perth, Western Australia, in 1993, as a 23-year-old who was broke and in desperate need of a job and an income. I had worked as a Xmas relief parcel delivery officer in Albany on the south coast of WA (where I was born) several years earlier, but I didn't really look upon it as something I wanted to pursue as a career, though I do remember the job being enjoyable all the same.

I owned very little after a trip to Europe in 1991 that had drained my finances, and I was relying on a bit of seasonal tennis coaching to pay the rent, living from pay to pay. I had travelled to Europe to try my luck on the French Tennis Money Circuit, but that didn't exactly net me huge dollars; in fact, around 4,000 French francs (Euros) was about the extent of my earnings, which equated to about a thousand bucks Australian, half the cost of my return flight.

(I did, however, leave French soil with a European Men's Doubles title won in the French countryside with my good mate PJ, and let's face it, not every tennis player, let alone a postie, can lay claim to that. The lion's share of the French francs I earned came from that tournament win.)

Something, however, made me look back to my time at the Albany Post Office where I worked in the late '80s, and I had only fond memories of the work I did there. It was only by chance that I stumbled across the job; the president of my local tennis club, Wally, asked me one day at club tennis if I was interested in doing some parcel deliveries, as he also just happened to be the local Postmaster.

Wally, who has since passed on, was responsible for my first experience working in the postal industry. Thanks Wally, RIP mate.

I vividly recall the posties rolling out early each day on their pushbikes and motorcycles and seeing them clock off most days around 1pm, though on a quiet day they were finished well before lunch.

That, to me, was a good enough reason to pursue the idea. Early start, early finish, enough time in the day to play golf, teach and play tennis, go to the beach, have a life outside of work. How many workplaces offer that?

I made just two phone calls:

The first was a no-go, but on the second one I hit the jackpot; the boss told me to come in the next day and see him as they were looking for relief workers to deliver Xmas mail on pushbikes. I believe it was a Thursday that I rode my pushbike in for a fairly casual interview, where I handed him a reference from Wally, and he asked me to start the following Monday.

(That's how easy it was to get a job back then; they were pretty much just a phone call away.)

I would spend the next eight years at The Post Office before heading back to the south coast of WA once more for another fifteen years of delivery, both bike and van.

'Kenny'

On day one I was introduced to the team at The Post Office, and they all seemed to be a good bunch of blokes with a combined sense of humour that I could relate to immediately. After introductions, Kenny basically 'claimed' me as he told the rest of the crew, "He's my boy and he's coming out with me today!"

(After thirty-three-plus years, my memory still disturbs me: how I can remember certain things that were said back then, word for word. But that's how much of an impression the place left on me.)

Kenny was a happy-go-lucky type of bloke with a very casual attitude towards life. I was to learn his delivery round so he could then act as another relief postie of sorts to help the other guys where required.

From day one, I could see I was going to be busy from the number of letters and cards being sorted by the guys at a pace I was in awe of.

(Aah yes, the good old-fashioned way of communicating.)

Kenny and I took what initially felt like way too much mail out with us on pushbikes and bundled the rest of the round's mail into some relay bags which were delivered to a halfway point to load up from once we'd run out.

I noticed the system from day one was fairly simple to decipher.

A postie could only take out so much mail, particularly on a pushbike compared to a motorbike, so more relay bags were required on the pushbike rounds. As explained, it felt like way too much mail because the carry bag on the front of the bike felt like someone had placed three or four bricks in it.

I can still remember following Kenny and noticing he owned calves resembling those of a weightlifter, no doubt carved out by regularly pushing the equivalent of three or four bricks on a pushbike for several hours each weekday. From memory, I don't believe I even wore a bike helmet, as I'm certain that back then they weren't compulsory, so a cap and plenty of sunscreen were usually the only requirements.

I kept up with Kenny pretty well as he showed me a trick or two as far as delivery was concerned, which essentially came down to concentrating on every number and street address and making certain I hadn't turned into the wrong street. (It's been done, believe me, as I've explained later in this book.)

Some rounds were done solely on a pushbike, though it's not to say they couldn't be done on a motorbike; the order of delivery simply required it to be set up differently back on the sorting table at the office. In other words, if a postie decided to do a motorcycle delivery round on a pushbike, the last street of a motorcycle round would be the first street delivered on a pushbike.

Pretty simple, the complete reverse due to opposite-hand delivery.

I found the whole thing outrageously appealing from the start, due to the simplicity of it all. That's not to say there wasn't an art to it; however, that art wasn't rocket science. Rather, it was more common sense. Not that I owned a lot back then, although I was keen to develop it.

I also saw the casual aspect of it.

By that I mean: here you were on a pushbike, something most human beings look upon as a leisure activity, yet it's also something that can be used as a vehicle for a delivery service. You are your own boss once you're out there, and all you have to do is stay upright, put a letter or magazine into a letterbox and not get run over in the process when crossing a busy street, and do it with a smile.

OK, the smile was optional. Still is. Though I highly recommend it.

Remember that classic Oz movie *The Castle*? Well, if you saw it, what was that famous saying in the movie? "It's all about the vibe." Same with the postie gig. If the sun was out, the birds were singing and deliveries were going well, it was one hell of a good vibe.

Rainy days, however, were a little more testing of the sense of humour.

Around half an hour or so into our deliveries, we made it to a business section of shops where we parked our bikes. Kenny grabbed the mail for a business and said, "Follow me, I want you to meet someone," as we entered a deli. He walked straight up to the front counter, grabbed a foot-long confectionery snake, stuffed it into his mouth and, while chewing on it, introduced me to the guy behind the counter.

As we shook hands, Kenny grabbed another snake and asked, "Here, you want one?!" Out of respect for the shop attendant I declined, but thought to myself that I could get used to this type of work as it was outrageously appealing in many ways; a bit of fitness, some banter with customers, and a sense of achievement after putting a jigsaw puzzle of sorts together.

I loved that first day on the delivery with Kenny, as it was a day's work like no other I had ever experienced, though Kenny's personality had a lot to do with my enjoyment, he was a character, no doubt about it.

He took over as the team leader once our long-serving captain of the ship, 'Leapy', moved into a managerial position and he did a fantastic job. He was Leapy's best buddy and they were both tarred with the same brush as far as sense of humour and work ethic were concerned. Kenny was about as shy as a rock star walking into a packed stadium. He could talk the leg off a chair and owned no shame whatsoever in anything he said or did.

Hey Kenny, thanks for showing me the ropes, and one more thing, I still owe you ten bucks, as the very next day after you showed me that delivery round, one of your customers gave me a tenner (true story) for being "such a great postie all year."

Aah, the benefits of being a relief postie at Xmas time. Owe you a beer, buddy...

'Leapy'

I have mentioned my original team leader from The Post Office on more than one occasion in this book regarding his leadership skills, but I cannot speak highly enough of him as a genuine human being.

Leapy took a few blokes from rags to riches, so to speak, through his generosity and more or less offered them a career in delivering mail, as he did with me. (Back then, the system was a little different to say the least, as basically you could offer a job to a mate, if, of course, you could trust them to do a good job, as your reputation as a team leader or boss would be on the line.)

Although Leapy did not take the initial phone call from me when I was looking for work, he did have the final say, as he was the one who mentored us posties and helped with our growth in every way he could.

During the initial three-month trial period of learning the job and basically doing our best to make the grade, it was Leapy who made decisions that would ultimately either make us or break us.

Personally, I went through much frustration initially on the motorcycle as my delivery times didn't really pick up too much from that of the pushbike.

"There's an art to it, mate, we will get you up to speed, trust me," Leapy assured me.

That's when he organised for our chief relief postie, Col, to go out on a round with me and show me some tricks of the trade. Leapy wasn't the sort of bloke who would just say something like, "Don't worry about it, you will get it eventually," rather, he made things happen for someone who was struggling.

That was his nature, just a ripper bloke.

A team leader's job is never easy, and Leapy is testimony to that fact, as he once had to revive a postie who had collapsed one morning. It happened prior to my days there, but it is by all reports in The Post Office folklore book of stories, and it proved that the position of looking after the team was a priority, which also included health issues.

According to more than one witness, whilst waiting for the ambulance to arrive, Leapy performed mouth-to-mouth on an ailing postie and on regaining consciousness, the postie in question vomited, and unfortunately for Leapy, well, you can picture the rest.

Now that's taking a hit for the team.

On another subject: I am sure Leapy won't mind me saying so, even though he is and has been happily married for many years, but as far as lacking confidence with the ladies was concerned, he really held no fear.

I passed him one morning at a local newsagency as he was dropping off some relay bags and we both glanced at an attractive lady as she entered the store. Rather than shy away from an opportunity, he smiled at the woman and came out with something along the lines of, "And a lovely morning to you," or words to that effect.

Amidst the ensuing light banter, Leapy came out with these words of wisdom: "Well you just never know, do you hey? You just never know," referring to the obvious fact that if you remain silent and don't offer so much as a greeting, then the chances of finding a future ten-pin bowling partner are fairly slim.

Leapy was the ringleader of a chosen few known as *The Breakfast Club*, who managed small pushbike and walk rounds, plus they owned a knack of finishing at ridiculously early times. They would often be seen having brekky at a local café which, looking back, was no doubt a way to blow their delivery times out, no risk at all.

Kenny and Phil would often be seen with Leapy downing a coffee and some bacon and eggs, with their postie pushbikes leaning up against a rail out the front of a café. Those three were as thick as thieves and drew much light-hearted abuse from the rest of us at The Post Office the next day if ever we spotted them relaxing while the rest of us were working.

Leapy, however, deserved it, he was worth his weight in gold.

His mail sorting prowess and speed would have you glancing his way on many occasions in awe, and I often likened his form to one of those cash-counting machines at a casino. If I had to describe his mail sorting, it would be summed up in one word: brilliant.

I have seen some in charge who go through the motions without making certain situations more comfortable for an employee who may have been struggling in a particular area, but not Leapy. He made the job fun, he made you want to get better at it, and he taught me that if ever I see a pretty woman, say g'day.

You never know. You just never know...

The 'Wary' Customer

Some customers are rather reluctant to open their front door, whereas some have asked me to take an item inside and leave it in a certain place for them, as if they've known me as a friend for years. Today's society is a little different than back in the '70s, however, and I certainly don't blame people for being wary.

It can make it a bit difficult though to offload a parcel if they are non-trusting of someone at their front door.

Here's a typical example of the *wary* customer:

"Hi there, Mrs Jones?"

"Yes."

"It's the postie, I have a parcel for you."

(Crickets. Nothing. No words. Just complete silence.)

"Soooooo would you like me to leave the parcel here for you, or would you like to open the door a little bit thanks, and I can hand it to you?"

"I suppose."

It's then that the door opens, but sometimes it only opens a little bit and not far enough to get the parcel inside.

"If you open the door a little more, thanks, Mrs Jones, I can give you the parcel, or I can simply leave it here for you on your doorstep."

Personally, if I get a knock on the door, someone is standing there wearing a high-viz shirt, holding a scanner, their van or motorcycle is parked in my driveway and I was expecting a delivery, well, I may just jump to the reasonably safe conclusion that it may in fact be the postie who has arrived with my item, so I will welcome him or her with open arms, and for that matter, a wide-open door.

But that's just me.

Some deliveries, as I have stated regularly, simply take longer than others.

Chapter 6:
Postie School, Redirecting Mail, Wrong Street, Wrong House

Every postie has to graduate. It's like life in general, you have to start somewhere and eventually you have to meet a standard set by management. After my initial start at The Post Office for the Xmas rush in '93, where I learned the basics, I was sent to Postie School to iron out any deficiencies or bad habits I may have picked up. Postie School is where careers begin and where the system offers advice, a bit like when you first learn to drive.

Let's face it, once you pass a driving test, you can drive however you like as long as it falls within certain guidelines, and it's the same as being a postie really, when all is said and done. You get taught the basics, but everyone has their own way of executing the finer points.

A bloke by the name of Dave took me and a young recruit out into suburbia and showed us both how to deliver a letter into a letterbox without falling off or running into parked cars. Yes, it was just the two of us; perhaps staffing turnover was slow at the time, but that's how it was during that week of training. Dave and two students, quite possibly one of his easier weeks of teaching.

Dave had a funny way of talking; nice bloke, but he always said the word *OK* in his own Dave sort of way: *Hockay* was how it came out. I recall speaking to another postie mate years later and he told me the same story:

"You had *Hockay Dave* as your trainer too, ey??!!"

Dave left an impression on more than one of us posties, without a doubt.

At Postie School it's imperative to listen, learn, and observe the main man or woman teaching you. It may seem easy at first glance, but believe me, there are issues involved that you'd never even consider at the beginning.

After a trip to a forest on the outskirts of town where we rode through soft sand and other obstacles, my bike falling over more than once, Dave noticed something about the other student that I didn't really take much notice of, as I was concentrating on staying upright: their ability (or rather, inability) to lift a fallen bike.

Dave put both our bikes on the ground, gently of course, and said, "There you go. If your bike ever falls over, which it will, whether you're an experienced postie or not, show me how you'd pick it up."

I thought to myself, *Is this a trick question??*

So I went over to my bike and simply picked it up. Dave said, "Good job."

The other student was slight in build, maybe 50 kilos at best, and Dave's request quickly turned into an epic. If I'd had my lunch with me, I honestly reckon I could've downed a round of sandwiches while watching it all unfold.

To cut a long story short, the bike never got picked up, no matter how hard the student tried. In a nutshell, that student never passed Postie School. As harsh as it seemed at the time, looking back it was obvious, it's not as though you can ring the office every time the bike falls over and ask:

"Me again, any chance you could head out and help me lift my bike up thanks, Boss?"

(For the record, I lost count of how many times my Honda 110 tipped over that day, but at least I could pick it up.)

So for the next two days it was just me and Dave, and it was the best fun I've ever had with my clothes on while learning a new job. Dave was brilliant, a funny guy with a warped sense of humour that I had no trouble relating to.

We collected some mail from a delivery centre on those two days and Dave showed me how to deliver it without chewing up manicured lawns or bowling over pedestrians on footpaths, plus he threw in a few etiquette suggestions when dealing with customers.

At one stage we stopped at a deli to grab a drink. We parked the bikes, Dave bought me a can of coke, and we sat on the ground outside the deli like a couple of homeless people. Dave talked to me about the job, dogs, customers, the weather, management, and how much he loved what he did.

I was fascinated from the very start, especially by the way Dave described the work.

Looking back, as I often do, Dave was right. He was teaching newbies to become part of a neighbourhood, part of suburbia, and an integral part of society. How could his job not be enjoyable? It was like teaching a kid to kick a footy, hit a tennis ball or belt a hockey ball, but with a bit more responsibility.

For the record, I passed Postie School. I reckon I did *hockay*.

Thanks, Dave.

The Redirection

There were many things about mail sorting and delivering that I'd never considered, like what happens when someone leaves an address and how their mail gets forwarded. I was told from day one that a redirection was NOT to be missed, though I wasn't really convinced as to why.

It basically went over my head because I was simply keen to make an impression, and by that, I mean I didn't want to be coming back to the office two hours after everyone else. That mindset can cause serious issues with a customer's mail, especially if they've already vacated the address.

I'll never forget the anxiety I felt watching all the posties head out on their deliveries after flying through their sorting process, which initially seemed like five minutes, while I was miles behind. Or rather, two hours behind, to be precise.

Each pigeonhole contained a redirection slip with the names and new addresses of customers who had shifted, or if their mail was to be put into a PO Box instead. Pretty simple stuff to follow.

Unless, of course, you were in a hurry.

I can honestly say this though: once you knew a delivery round well, you memorised the redirections rather than checking the slips. As soon as you reached a certain street on the sorting frame, you already knew that Mr Smith from number 5 had moved interstate, or Mrs Johnson from number 10 had moved two streets over, and her new address was documented.

When I first started in the 90s, those items were forwarded by writing the new address out yourself, which eventually gave way to redirection stickers once technology finally kicked in. Writing out new addresses was a lengthy exercise, particularly on a busy day where 40 or 50 items needed redirecting. There were also plenty of items that required a stamp that stated; *insufficient address* or *no such number.*

I am uncertain as to why I chose to ignore most of the slips initially, but all I remember was that I was concentrating on my sorting and trying to keep up with the rest of the guys, so the *insignificant* things were just that, insignificant as far as I was concerned.

I believe it took only a day or two before the list of customer complaints started rolling in and Boss Ted called me in for a chat.

"GT, we need to talk."

Now Ted was a good bloke, nice nature about him, and he didn't go off at me. He simply explained the importance of redirecting mail, as some households may have had a marriage split, and documents posted to, say, *Mr Jones*, who'd been given the red card, needed to be intercepted by the postie and sent elsewhere, as just one example.

I saw his point straight away and rectified the issue.

Now, I don't mean to blow my own trumpet here, but I will anyhow. About a year later, we had an in-office competition organised by a temporary boss after Ted left. He would take a month of information on all posties, good and bad, dissect the data, and award the title of *Postie of the Month.*

Half a carton of beer went to the postie doing the job with minimum fuss and, of course, with a minimum of customer complaints, and that meant NO REDIRECTION FAILURES.

Rather than bore you with all the details, I won the competition THREE MONTHS IN A ROW before management got wind of the fact that beer was being handed out to an employee. Some killjoy decided it was inappropriate and shut the whole idea down, but I looked back on those three months with a fair bit of pride. Not one redirection error in all that time, and from memory, I received at least one glowing customer recommendation, I think it was for dropping an elderly customer's mail on their doorstep one rainy day.

(That always earns a postie brownie points.)

I'd come a long way from my early days of upsetting customers with my lack of understanding, which attracted a list of complaints long enough to give me my own drawer in the boss's filing cabinet.

Ted, if you ever read this book mate, I got it together eventually, and I still hold the record for *Postie of the Month*. I'm certain I could've won a couple more through the year if some miserable bastard hadn't pulled the pin on the new office incentive.

I'll always go the extra mile if a beer is up for grabs.

Wrong Street

On any given day something can go wrong if a postie numbers their bundles of letters or oversized articles incorrectly, or even heads down the wrong street if they're still unfamiliar with an area. I once made a major mess of my deliveries by grabbing the wrong bundle of mail, and it cost me a bit of time, and a lot of frustration.

I was well into my first month or so of being a postie and I'd sorted my round to perfection, or at least I assumed so, and was all fired up for another day of delivering on the pushbike. The round I was doing at the time had two streets with very similar names, or at least similar enough in the way I perceived them.

To cut a long story short, I delivered about half a bundle of letters, A4 envelopes and magazines into the letterboxes of the wrong street.

How? Simple.

I grabbed the wrong bundles.

What actually gave it away was that, towards the second half of the street, a few letters didn't match the numbers on the letterboxes and I started scratching my head. But generally, let's face it, most streets start the same as far as numbers go. It only changes once unit numbers appear, or an A, B or C address pops up. Without units, most streets are numbered pretty much the same.

Looking back, I probably had a letter for, say, 21A and didn't find a 21A, so I just delivered it to 21 instead because I was naive and still learning the job, plus I could've sworn I was in the right street. But once I saw more than one wrongly numbered item failing to match the letterboxes, the alarm bells started ringing.

After realising the mistake, I quickly backtracked and pulled as many letters and magazines out of letterboxes as I could before customers emptied them. Unfortunately, some had already collected their mail. After knocking and explaining, they handed the mail back.

Some letterboxes were bomb-proof with locks on them, so if the customers weren't home, I had to write them a note on a card explaining the problem and asking if they could please put the mail back into the red post box down the road, for pick-up and correct delivery the following day by the idiot postie.

(No, I didn't write that much detail on the card, but the thought crossed my mind.)

I learned my lesson from that little exercise, which cost me about an hour. From that day onwards, especially in that area, I wrote a few extra details on each bundle of mail so I wouldn't get confused again. It always pays to say it out loud sometimes at the start of a street as you grab a bundle of mail, just in case.

If, as a customer, you've ever received a letter or magazine with a number written on it that has nothing to do with your house number, well, mystery solved. It was probably the order number of your postie's bundle.

For any newbie postie, a bit of simple advice: don't assume you know where you are. Look at the street sign and then the bundle of letters before you start delivering. Reasonably basic advice, yet things can go pear-shaped very quickly if the process isn't followed correctly, especially for a new employee.

Every postie in the world has made an error one way or another, they wouldn't be human if they hadn't, but it's all about the magnitude of the f… up that can define you as a postie.

I'm testimony to that fact.

Wrong House

Delivering mail to the wrong house is usually no one's fault but the postie's, either due to a lack of concentration during delivery or because it was sorted incorrectly back at the office. However, there is another way a letter, magazine, or parcel can end up at the wrong address, kids. Yes, that's right, kids.

So how does it happen?

From day one at Postie School, Dave went through the dos and don'ts of delivering mail, and there was quite a list, trust me. One of them is this: **DON'T GIVE MAIL TO KIDS.** I suppose it's up to the postie to decide if a child is old enough to take the mail to their parents when they are standing in the front yard with an outstretched hand.

If they aren't at the 'responsible' age, then maybe the letter you handed to them at the letterbox one day didn't make it to mum or dad for one reason or another. There are plenty of things a young kid could do with their parents' mail instead of handing it to them, so rather than risk it, it's usually smarter to either put the item in the letterbox yourself or take it to the front door.

At least that way, if the property has a security camera, which many do nowadays, mum or dad can see that you did your job before a child moved the item elsewhere. Here's a situation I faced very early in my postie career:

I arrived at an address where a young kid was at the letterbox, holding out their hand for the mail. So here I was, faced with a situation that the Postie School Zen Master Dave had warned me about from day one, and I had a decision to make:

1. Should I heed his advice?

2. Should I leave it to my own discretion, which I thoroughly believed in?

Yep, I went with number two. I thought, it'll be fine.

This is what happened:

I gave the letter to the kid, who grabbed it with a huge smile and ran straight across the road to his house! The address he was waiting at wasn't his. He had obviously watched me ride past his house earlier in disappointment because I didn't have any mail for them, so he moved to the other side of the road to get some.

Ingenious. That kid has probably gone far in life, or he's in jail for stealing.

I wheeled my bike across the road, knocked on the door, spoke to his mum, explained the situation, and she handed me the letter and even apologised. I told her it was my fault and that I should have known better. As I rode off, I thought back to when I was a kid and my mum or dad would say things like, "Don't touch that, it's hot" or "Make sure you put sunscreen on or you will get burnt."

You know it yourself; the list is endless.

I ate humble pie that day. The main man of Postie School had seen it all before, but I was five minutes into the job and apparently knew everything. To Dave, the Zen Master of Postie School, you were right, mate. My apologies for doubting you. I learned my lesson the hard way; it didn't happen again.

The 'Non-Believing' Customer

This one can be a headache for a postie, particularly on a busy day when time is tight. It has happened to me many times, especially on van deliveries when I arrived with a parcel. Some customers simply cannot accept that they have an item addressed to them, and a typical conversation might go like this:

"Hi there Mrs Jones, I have a parcel for you. Do you mind signing for it, thanks?"

"What is it? I haven't ordered anything."

"Not sure, Mrs Jones, but lucky you, a surprise. Just a signature, thanks, if you don't mind."

Mrs Jones then inspects the item like a CSI bomb disposal expert looking for the red wire to cut.

"Well, it may be a gift, Mrs Jones. Is it your birthday? Any chance of a signature, thanks?"

"No, it's not my birthday. I wonder who on earth sent me something?"

Then the waiting game begins as Mrs Jones examines the item, maybe even sniffs it. I have had many customers at their door refuse to accept that someone might have sent them a gift. This type of customer is always a challenge and can be frustrating when they ignore requests for a signature.

On more than one occasion, I've had to give a customer an ultimatum:

"Look, please excuse me, but I really have to keep moving. If you aren't 100 percent sure it's for you, I can return it to the sender if you like."

Usually, this gets a signature, but not always. So, has a customer ever refused to sign for an item? Yes, one or two over the years. Sometimes it's because the item was incorrectly addressed, or the customer was unsure of the legitimacy of the delivery. The scanners offered an option for 'Customer Refusal' so the item could be scanned and returned to the sender.

Glenn Thompson

I was always a big fan of non-signature items, for obvious reasons.

70

Chapter 7:
Some Real Characters
and GT's Delivery Round

'Kurt' was without a doubt one of the funniest blokes I had ever met; a real character with a highlight reel as long as Gary Ablett's AFL career. I recall the first day I turned up at The Post Office, and Kurt was larger than life, loud, obnoxious, and very, very funny.

He was a fitness fanatic who had legs like tree trunks, carved from his obsession with riding his pushbike around 18 kilometres from home to the office just for a warm-up before his deliveries.

Back then, if you were employed as a pushbike delivery officer, it wasn't necessary to switch to a motorbike. This suited many guys who didn't want to change. I spent my first two months on a pushbike, though it was temporary as I was expected to get a motorcycle licence as soon as possible, which I eventually did to save my legs three to four hours of mail delivery each day.

Some guys loved the pushbike, like Kurt. Personally, I found it physically draining. Each to their own. Kurt was so hyped after his epic daily ride into work that he was like a wind-up toy with long-life batteries that refused to slow down.

I was lucky enough to secure a spot next to him on a sorting bay from day one and he would have me in stitches with his humour, especially during primary sorting. Sometimes Kurt would turn over a postcard to check who was sending what and give me a running commentary on the picture, particularly if it featured a scantily clad woman, which we saw plenty of on postcards.

I vividly recall one morning after a rain-affected ride into work when Kurt walked from the lunchroom into the main sorting area with a pair of motorcycle gloves on his feet because his socks and shoes were wet; he had taken them off to dry.

"Kurt, shoes on!" Team Leader Leapy said, trying to assert some authority, though the loud laughter around the office made it difficult. Have you ever tried wearing gloves on your feet? It takes a bit of skill, but Kurt had most silly things down to an art form.

Leapy had gone out early one morning to deliver his round, and we were all playing up a bit, like you used to when your schoolteacher left the classroom. Burns opened the back door of the office to take his mail out, and Kurt seized the opportunity to ride his pushbike into the delivery room and do a lap around the office before heading out to deliver his mail.

That was just the sort of thing he did.

He also owned a bit of nous when it came to postie/dog interaction. A tennis ball or two were wedged into the frame of his pushbike so that if he saw a dog running towards him, he would throw the ball in a different direction. 'Survival methods' he told me.

Kurt also had a rather large say in what radio station we listened to while we were going through a bit of a transition about what we should tune in to daily. He dismantled the tuning system so the radio station could not be changed from the one he liked. We only found that out several weeks later when the cleaner spilled the beans. Apparently, Kurt had gone into the office one Saturday morning and told the cleaner he was there to 'fix' the radio.

I still remember the innocent look on his face when we were all quizzing each other about what had happened to the radio and why the station could no longer be changed.

I took a liking to Kurt from day one. He was a fairly likeable bloke, and some of the things he would come out with defied any type of logic. One morning he showed me a dog magazine with a picture of a dachshund (sausage dog) on the front cover and told me it was a 'fully worked' and 'lowered' dog, in reference to a hotted-up car that had its springs lowered at the front. Only a very unique mind could come up with something like that.

He was a different type of human being, no doubt about it. Someone once told us that Kurt went to a weekend retreat to 'find himself' and when he came back, well, he was a bit hard to handle. Whatever they taught him that weekend obviously helped with his lively attitude towards life, which I found infectious, for want of a better word.

I was called into the boss's office one morning because I had made another redirection error, and he told me I had to stop talking so much to Kurt as he was obviously distracting me. He was very correct, but trying to explain that to Kurt was like trying to tell a mate you didn't want another beer.

Kurt quizzed me on the trip to the boss's office and when I explained the dialogue to him, he just laughed and carried on talking to me non-stop until we had finished sorting our rounds.

On a totally unrelated postal matter, I went into the city one afternoon by train with Kurt and Burns, just for something to do. After lunch, we took different trains back home. Just as Burns boarded his train, Kurt yelled out, "Hey Burns, don't forget to get that STD of yours sorted before it gets any worse!"

I still wonder how the passengers on that train looked at Burnsey for the rest of the trip after Kurt had put that one out there for all to hear.

The day Kurt left The Post Office to pursue a career elsewhere was a bit of a sad day, even though at times he rubbed a few people up the wrong way with his antics. Like an energizer bunny whose batteries never ran out, that was Kurt.

One of a kind you were mate...

'Carlos'

This guy was in a hurry with just about everything he did, and it wasn't just confined to the workplace; Carlos simply owned zero patience. We played tennis a few times, and he would usually count to three shots then BOOM, a winner was attempted. I suggested he should try to have a rally more often, but that always fell on deaf ears.

I pulled up behind him at a petrol station one morning as we rolled in to fill up our motorbikes before delivery. It was like watching a scene from a MotoGP race. I have never seen a guy fill a tank so quickly, run inside to sign for the fuel, then get back on his bike and take off as though he was racing Valentino Rossi.

I watched in awe and asked him one day, "Mate, what's the hurry? You're always in a rush. Got somewhere you need to be?"

"Gotta get home and do stuff. No point in dragging the day out any longer than I have to."

I thought, yep, fair call.

Being in a hurry, though, could get you into strife as a postie. Carlos was spoken to by our team leader one morning over an incident that could only be described as 'Carlos being Carlos'.

Back in the early 1990s, it was rare to receive a letter on your delivery round that required a signature. (It was called registered mail, or a 'regie'.) On some weeks, a postie could go without delivering more than one or two per day, and it wasn't unusual to have two or three days without any at all, which made deliveries a lot quicker.

It was always a bit of a drag having to knock on a door, wait for the customer to answer, write out their information in a book (scanners do this now), and get a signature before leaving. For a guy like Carlos, a registered item went down about as well as a fish milkshake and you could hear the cogs turning in his mind when he received one or two in the morning as to how he could create a shortcut on delivery.

On certain delivery rounds a reasonable distance from the main office, an adjoining newsagency that owned a postal outlet would be used as the base for registered letters if the customer wasn't home. There was nothing worse than having to backtrack at the end of deliveries if the main office wasn't the preferred collection point. This could mean a dead ride of a few kilometres for one letter, something Carlos was not at all prepared to do if he could help it.

I will never forget the day Carlos decided to create a shortcut. He wrote a card for the customer back at the office and then took the registered letter to a newsagency early in his deliveries, eliminating the need to backtrack if the customer wasn't home.

That would have worked beautifully if the customer had been out shopping, but in this case, 'Mrs Smith' was home and waiting outside at her letterbox, as many customers often did. The scenario played out like this:

Carlos handed 'Mrs Smith' a card (Sorry We Missed You), even though he hadn't missed her at all as it's hard to miss someone waiting at their letterbox. The card explained the process that Mrs Smith had to follow to collect her item from the postal outlet that was perhaps a couple of kilometers from her house.

All of this was explained to not only Carlos but the rest of us the following morning by Team Leader Leapy:

"Carlos, it makes it tough to build a case for you if you hand a customer a card that explains how to collect an item due to them not being home, even though they were obviously home as you hand delivered it to them! Just wondering, in a hurry, were you?"

As already explained, Leapy was a ripper bloke to have as a team leader, as fair as you like. He would let you know that if you messed up once, it probably shouldn't happen twice, particularly when it came to registered mail. I think Carlos learned his lesson.

If he signed off at 12.30 pm, it wasn't all bad, even though his preferred sign-off time was 12 pm. He had his sorting and delivery down to an art form and was more or less a part-timer compared to the rest of us, who didn't mind working until 1 pm.

Carlos and I once swapped delivery rounds to see who could deliver one another's the quickest. I felt I was a fair chance to beat him as he wasn't familiar with my area however I knew his delivery round as I had delivered it once or twice.

After comparing finishing times the following day, it was fairly easy to decipher that Carlos beat me by the proverbial 'country mile'. In fact, I believe that Carlos completed my delivery round, made it back to his house and finished his lunch before I even made it back to the office.

I was simply not in his league.

Carlos is still working for Oz Post to this day, still in a hurry, and still looking for a shortcut, by all reports.

'Hammy'

Before I get into Hammy's profile, I honestly still don't know what sort of postie he was, or still is, to tell the truth. I was told he's still on a bike somewhere over east. What I do know is this: Hammy was without a doubt one of the highlights of The Post Office each morning.

I learned during Hammy's tenure that some people in life you simply cannot beat in an argument, no matter your intelligence level, and sometimes it's easier to admit defeat than put yourself through pointless frustration.

One of Hammy's finest moments came in the form of a footy tipping competition.

Just prior to a new AFL season, Carlos and I decided a footy tipping comp was something the office needed. Tipping winners in our national game created a bit of banter and bravado on a Monday morning.

"You tipped Fitzroy to beat Collingwood? What were you thinking, you nitwit?"

That was in fact me, the 'nitwit' who made some rather silly decisions with my tipping. Looking back, Fitzroy barely won a game, so I deserved all the criticism I received for picking them on any given week.

We charged $4 per week, which not only guaranteed a reasonable weekly prize of around $25–$30, but also built a tidy sum at the end of the season for the gun tipster of the year. Fair to say, there were a few dollars lying around in a jar that Carlos and I would occasionally borrow from to buy morning tea, a drink, or perhaps lunch.

Let's be clear, we DID NOT STEAL the footy tipping money. It was impossible to do so, as everything was documented from the start of the season about how much would be paid weekly and at the end of it all. But let's also be honest here: we were paid fortnightly, and sometimes towards the end of that two-week pay cycle, someone would be short of a dollar.

Hammy was a man of principal without a doubt and he could be hilarious at times but also a complete pain in the arse, yet he made us all laugh with his staunch views on certain subjects. I don't remember who let the cat out of the bag, but looking back, it was rather silly of either myself or Carlos to mention anything within earshot of Hammy that could perhaps ruffle his feathers.

"What was that you guys? You are borrowing from the footy tipping money to service your own needs? OK, I want to borrow five bucks then."

I believe it was Carlos who asked the obvious question:

"Why, what do you want it for?"

"None of your business. I want five bucks, and I want it by the end of the day, thanks fellas," Hammy replied.

Carlos and I looked at each other and shrugged. Yep, Hammy had a point. If we were stupid enough to admit borrowing from the slush fund, then we had to lend to others supposedly 'in need'. One of us opened the jar and handed Hammy a fiver, which he placed on his sorting bay for everyone to see.

The next day it was still there. And the day after that. In fact, the $5 note sat there for almost a week. Carlos and I asked Hammy several times:

"Hey Hammy, the fiver is still on your sorting bay. What are you doing with it?"

"None of ya business," was Hammy's regular response.

After about a week, Carlos and I decided to get the fiver back into the footy tipping kitty. We counted the money and showed Hammy, down to the last dollar, what should be in the pool. We suggested he also pay back the five bucks, which he did.

From that day on, we never borrowed another cent from the footy tipping kitty (not that we told anyone about anyhow), particularly Hammy. We weren't prepared to go through the intense interrogation from him again as he was onto us about that personal loan like a seagull onto a chip.

Hammy was brilliant in many areas and I believe that no one ever won an argument against him! He was streets ahead of most of us as far as current affairs were concerned and some of his answers had us in awe of his knowledge.

He also had a brilliant take on holidays. I will never forget the day we were filling out a holiday form, writing down our preferred month off. Hammy came out with this little chestnut:

"You know the best day of your holidays, fellas? The Friday before you even start."

He elaborated:

"The equation is simple. You have several hours at the end of your delivery round on Friday before the weekend even starts, time to ponder your upcoming break. Then you have two days to go before your holidays officially kick off. In my opinion, the Friday before the following Monday when your holidays start is the best day of your holidays. Think about that."

And so we did. I've used that theory for 30-odd years.

Thanks Hammy, genius you were. I hope you're educating the posties at your new office as well as you educated us blokes back in the day on the morals of life.

GT's Delivery Round (Shop Boy)

During my time at The Post Office, I was assigned to 5 or 6 of the 10 delivery rounds, as we would change rounds yearly. I did, however, spend the last three or so years on the same delivery round because no one else wanted it.

It was the business district round.

Carlos spent just one day on that round before coming back to the office cursing like a disgruntled salesman who didn't land a deal. He tore strips off the whole idea of swapping rounds. That's when I put my thinking cap on, which seemed to happen quite regularly in my new workplace. Perhaps it was the challenge of solving daily issues that agreed with my silly mind. Whatever it was, I enjoyed and embraced most challenges.

I was rather disappointed that I had to move one seat along in January of that year (probably 1998) because I didn't entirely love the Honda 110, though I liked it a lot more than the bicycle, which stripped me of valuable kilograms. I loved the morning walk through the business district, talking to shop owners and employees alike. To me, that was the most enjoyable part of delivering mail, the social aspect.

The business district delivery round was a half-and-half style round (half walk, half bike) where the priority was to get the business mail sorted and delivered as early as possible. Most days I would sort the business mail, load up the trolley, and do the brisk walk, which could be done in around 45 minutes on a quiet day, or about 90 minutes on a busy day.

Then I would walk back to the office, sort the mail for the other half of the round, which I did on the Honda, then head out for another 90 minutes or so on average.

On small mail volume days, I would sort the product for both halves of the round before the shop deliveries, so when I got back to the office after the walk, I basically just jumped on the bike and headed off as I already had the mail sorted; all I had to do was load it, which was a five-minute job.

You were your own boss, so you could vary the daily system, providing it was efficient, however the business deliveries were the earliest daily priority. As long as they were completed first, management and business owners alike were happy.

Anyhow, the conversation between Carlos and myself started something like this as he vented his spleen: "F... that round. I have no interest whatsoever in prancing around the shops with a trolley looking like an ice cream vendor".

In fact, I think those were Carlos' exact words. I saw a chance to get my favourite round back and told Carlos I would do my best to sort the issue.

It was then that I floated the idea to Team Leader Leapy that Carlos should perhaps move to my new round, a complete motorcycle round with no walking involved, and that I stay on the shop delivery round for obvious reasons. We needed to keep the harmony going, and if Carlos became the new 'shop boy,' the whole vibe of the office, and in particular the business district at delivery time, would take a nose dive of epic proportions.

Leapy agreed. Having Carlos deliver the business district mail would have been a public relations disaster. He was a bloody good postie, but his skill set was basically confined to bike delivery. Becoming the new shop boy involved a little more patience, a slower paced delivery, and of course, talking to customers, which he didn't like doing because he was always in a hurry.

On finding out he was to bypass the shop delivery round, Carlos' mood swung to that of a happy camper who had just toasted his marshmallows to perfection over a campfire. I think he may have even thanked me, which I didn't receive much of over the years from Carlos regarding anything I did for him.

I kept the 'shop boy' tag that everyone had pretty much given me from day one when I was assigned to shop mail deliveries. The Post Office kept the good vibes going, just like the Beach Boys sang back in the 70's and that was pretty much my job description for my final three years at The Post Office.

Good, good, good, good vibrations...

The 'Park in front of your Letterbox' Customer

As I've explained elsewhere in this book, on average, most posties have anywhere between 1,000 and 1,500 letterboxes to deliver to each day.

All they ask is that customers show a bit of intelligence about where they park their cars.

If you've ever received your mail under the windscreen wiper of your car, this may shed some light on it.

Believe it or not, when I started as a postie in 1993, I was taught to place mail under the windscreen wiper if a vehicle was parked in front of a letterbox on a regular basis. I'm talking about someone who made a habit of blocking deliveries, not a one-off situation.

This was well before online shopping took off, and the majority of deliveries were letters and magazines. The windscreen wiper idea was basically invented to deter people from parking in a postie's path.

I did it on several occasions, but never on a rainy day, for obvious reasons. Leaving someone's mail out in the rain probably wasn't the best idea for customer relations.

Did it work? Bloody oath it did.

If I ever left someone's mail under their windscreen wiper, I can guarantee that the very next day, if that vehicle was at the same premises, it wasn't parked in front of the letterbox. So, if you were ever involved in a 'windscreen wiper mail episode', there's some closure for you.

Chapter 8:
Days Off, The Radio and Payday

The Day Off

In the eight years I spent at The Post Office, I only had eight days off. I was reasonably fit and healthy, and I enjoyed going to work. Mostly because it was fun, guys like Kurt and Carlos made me laugh, and the unpredictable nature of the job meant every day was like a raffle. You never knew what would get dished up.

Towards the end of Kurt's time at the office, he started taking the piss even more than usual. I recall a really lousy day weather-wise when the phone rang around 5.55 am. It was Kurt. Burns took the call and relayed the message:

"Kurt won't be coming in today 'cos he's concerned about how windy it is. He reckons there's a chance he might get hit by a roof tile."

We all had a laugh at that one. A rather unique excuse for a day off, though Kurt was a unique human being, no doubt. I think he may have been grilled about it, but I don't think he cared much. He left The Post Office not long after, probably using up his sick days and inventing excuses. Funny bugger.

My desire to do the job well and make an impression among my new workmates began pretty early. There was no way I was letting a few stitches stop me from getting on the pushbike. Two weeks into the job, I ripped open my foot on a sprinkler while taking the bins out at home. It hurt like hell, looked serious, and blood was oozing everywhere.

I rang my doctor buddy Mick.

"Mick, it's GT. Bit of an issue, I've just opened up my heel on a sprinkler head while taking the bins out. A lot of blood. Think I need a stitch."

"Come around, I'll fix it."

I drove to Mick's place, where he removed the bandage and gave me the news:

"Yep, you need a stitch."

Ever had a needle in your heel? Makes your eyes water. Mick stitched me up, and I limped into work the next day, only my ninth or tenth day on the job.

Leapy asked the obvious question:

"Why are you limping?"

"Had a stitch in my heel. Should be OK, will just ride the pushy on one leg, no dramas."

Kurt came out later that day to check on me. He brought a motorbike after his pushbike round, took some mail off me, delivered it, and thanked me for coming in. I hadn't realised at the time how important it was for a postie to turn up, particularly on a Friday, the day most guys called in 'sick'.

I did pretty well that day, if I may say so myself. I leaned on the other leg a little more when riding up hills and did my best to keep pressure off the heel. That story got bolder over the years, sort of like the Monty Python skit where the soldier loses an arm or two and calls it 'merely a flesh wound'.

I took inspiration from that clip and told many a postie about the day I had to stop regularly to ring the blood out of my sock before continuing deliveries. (I didn't, but it sounded impressive.)

I did have a day off once because my beloved cat, Fatso, came to a grisly end under a car, and I was shattered. He meant the world to me. I rang Chris, the team leader at the time, and told him I was crook. Naturally, Chris being Chris questioned me:

"Waddaya mean you're crook? You're never crook."

Well, I was in no state to deliver mail that day. Some posties take a day off for family reasons, fair enough. I've had days off for the birth of my first child, which I considered a fair excuse. But I've rarely taken a day off for being legitimately sick, I just don't get sick, lucky, I guess.

When someone took a suspect day off, I'd revert back to the ripped heel story for interrogation the next day:

"You get over ya little ailment, champ? How's ya sniffle? Did I ever tell you about the time I went in to work on one leg?! Take a seat and I'll talk you through it."

And it got better every time I told it.

Crook as a Dog

On the other side of the coin, it is not a smart idea to completely disgrace yourself in front of your new workmates too early in the job. However, I honestly believe that my attempt to turn up to work while practically on one leg may have earned me a bit of goodwill.

It was only two or three weeks later that I decided to head out on a Sunday night to drown my sorrows at a pub after a relationship break-up. I could relate to the U2 song, "Until the end of the World," where they sing: *In my dreams I was drowning my sorrows, but my sorrows they learned to swim.*

That was me that Sunday night at the pub. I went hard, but nothing changed the next day. My sorrows were alive and kicking and I had more than four hours of pushbike deliveries to get through. I had only been at work for about an hour when I had to rush to the toilet to throw up the leftover beer from the night before.

Ted offered me a bit of sympathy after hearing me from his office.

"You're not too good, are you GT?"

"I'll be fine, Ted. I can only improve from here."

I managed to sort my mail, load the pushbike and head out on my round, but I was well behind schedule as the other guys had left at least an hour earlier. My head was pounding and tormenting me for being so stupid the night before work, especially in a new job.

I will never forget the relief I felt about an hour into my deliveries when Burns turned up on his Honda to take a good portion of my mail. I was forever grateful to him for helping me out; I was a trainwreck.

It always pays to build a bit of credit at work before you need your workmates to bail you out due to your own stupidity and a Sunday night drinking binge.

Legend, Burnsey.

The Radio

Every post office has a radio and ours was no different. The problem was that no one could agree on which station it should be tuned to and it sparked plenty of debate most days. Our radio was a very basic one, complete with a tape deck.

For anyone not old enough to know what a tape deck was, think of it as an early version of an iPod, although the tapes were notorious for getting caught in the player. Then you would spend ages winding the tape back in, usually with a pen. Great fun. Now and then someone brought in a tape, but only those brave enough to cop the abuse about their music taste. Most days we listened to a bland local station that played safe, non-offensive songs.

Personally, I was and still am a glam rock fan who loved anything with an edge and a few decent riffs. I only tried my luck once with a Def Leppard tape. Never again, I told myself after that disastrous effort.

Every track was met with: "What's this shit?"

Like I said, never again, and I stuck to it.

The radio at The Post Office was old and the stations always had a bit of static. We could never quite find the perfect spot on the dial for a clear signal. I will never forget the day it all came to a head.

Chris walked up to the radio one morning, lifted it off the shelf and smashed it on the floor! As we all stood up in complete shock, Kel, our team leader at the time, walked straight over to the debris with two elastic bands and wrapped them around the two biggest surviving pieces.

"It's alright. I think it will be fine," he said as he placed them back on the shelf.

You have never heard louder laughter at a situation that today would probably involve Head Office and a response team. Chris grabbed a broom, swept up the remains, tossed them in the bin and went straight back to sorting his mail like nothing had happened.

We eventually got a new radio a few weeks later. It had a better tuner and the big fella left it alone. He had already made his point.

The radio is an essential part of any post office. In fact, I reckon it is essential in any office. Working without background noise is eerie. Everyone relaxes more with a radio on and people do not whisper as much. That is a fact.

Try talking to the person next to you about your love life without a radio on and tell me honestly that you do not whisper. The radio has its advantages, you know it, I know it, we all know it.

Pay Day

I am not sure whether the boss at The Post Office even told me what I would be earning at the interview, but I didn't really care. I knew it would be more than what I was making at the time. I was working part time as a tennis coach at a local club and was paid fifteen dollars an hour to keep kids entertained on a tennis court.

It was not difficult work, but the hours were limited. In fact, I think the head coach could only offer me around twenty hours a week. You can do the sums on that pay cheque.

The postie job was surely going to bring in a bit more, although I had no idea how much more. Team Leader Leapy was as honest as he was down to earth and nothing was off limits, least of all how much each postie earned each fortnight. Leapy made a point on some pay days of letting the cat out of the bag.

Let me explain:

Each fortnight, usually a day before pay was deposited into our bank accounts, a green pay slip bag would arrive at each post office. Finding that among the mail some days felt like finding a gold nugget.

The funny thing was this: sometimes we would work what seemed to be the same hours as the previous fortnight yet get paid a different amount. In other words, we never received two identical pays, which filled pay week with much anticipation.

When the pay slip bag was found, mail sorting usually stopped while the slips were handed out. Whoever did the handing out also tended to glance at each one along the way as the slips were not in personalised envelopes.

From day one, Leapy told me, "Remember this, GT, a slow postie is a rich postie," although I had no idea what he meant. I did not even know my hourly rate. Overtime and meal allowances were never explained to me, though I often heard the other posties talking about them.

I was curious but did not ask too many questions, although I thought about it often until that first pay.

Overtime?

What is this thing called overtime and what on earth is a meal allowance?

Leapy found my pay slip and burst out laughing.

"Hey GT, remember what I told you about being a slow postie? Have a look at this."

I still remember the figure. I had cleared just over twelve hundred dollars for my first full fortnight on the job. It might not seem like much now, but consider this: it was double what I was earning hitting tennis balls to kids for twenty hours a week at fifteen bucks an hour. And six hundred a week in the early nineties was roughly equivalent to twice that now, maybe more.

My share of the rent back then was fifty dollars a week and from memory a carton of beer was around twenty to twenty-five dollars on special. So twelve hundred clear for a fortnight was like a small lotto win.

I took the payslip from Leapy, stared at it for a long time, then stared at it again and again before slipping it into my pocket and continuing with my sorting. I was floating, completely stunned by the biggest pay of my life.

Looking back, I was not trying to be a slow postie. I was simply learning the job. My sorting was nowhere near up to standard and if I made it back to the office before four o'clock each day it was a bonus, especially as I was doing it all on a pushbike.

I went to the bank the next day like a bloke who had just won Lotto, grinning like a cheshire cat and feeling a fresh enthusiasm for life. Sure, I was physically worn out most days, but I knew the pushbike would be gone sooner rather than later and maybe some of the overtime would drop off. Even so, I knew I was still going to be better off financially.

By age 24, I was finally earning a decent living, working in a highly entertaining workplace full of characters and enjoying every minute of it. Apart from Mondays and Tuesdays when mail volumes were reasonably heavy and an eleven-hour day was not uncommon, I was usually home by 2 pm and perhaps even 1pm on a Friday.

Life was looking up.

For the record, the postal industry eventually did away with the green pay slip bag in favour of personalised pay envelopes. Rumour had it that some posties, perhaps the slower ones, were not thrilled about their workmates knowing their fortnightly pay.

Most of us were devastated. Knowing what the bloke next to you earned led to some truly entertaining banter.

The 'Fortunate' Customer

Quite often, an item will come through the system with either an incorrect address or none at all, perhaps only a name. Finding the correct address could be a real challenge, and still is. In the old days, we would go through the phone book to match a surname and, more often than not, we found the right person.

When we finally located the correct address, the sense of achievement was enormous. It was always satisfying delivering something that easily could have been returned to sender.

I once received a box of chocolates from a very grateful customer whose parcel had been addressed to a number that did not exist. Her street only had even numbers and the opposite side of the road was bushland. Her parcel had an odd number written on it.

For example, she lived at 234 but the parcel was addressed to 235. Pretty simple mistake, but she was over the moon with the delivery, especially as she said the contents were quite expensive.

A switched-on postie usually learns the names as well as the house numbers, which can earn the occasional box of chocolates. But a postie new to a round will obviously lack that local knowledge, so a wrongly addressed item can be tricky to deliver.

If you are one of these fortunate customers, lucky you, because not every item reaches its destination. Some end up being returned to sender, which can cause frustration, yet sometimes it is the only option.

I worked with a local legend named Freddy on the south coast, my second Australia Post location, and Freddy was worth his weight in gold.

If a letter or parcel came through with an incorrect or missing address, we went straight to Freddy, who was a genius. Some items only had a name and a town or post code, nothing else, which made them nearly impossible to deliver.

I do not recall Freddy ever failing to work out where something belonged. And if he did not know the address, he would know exactly who to ask.

Freddy had a mind like an encyclopaedia for local knowledge.

I saw items come through with descriptions like:

John Smith, not sure of the number or street, three doors down from the police station and owns a bull terrier. That is all I know.

As long as the post code was correct and the description was at least halfway useful, the recipient might still receive their item and be counted among the fortunate customers.

P.S Don't forget to thank your postie for their detective work if they have tracked you down on an incorrectly addressed item. An item marked as insufficient or incorrect address can mean a potential week or two turn-around, particularly if it's travelling interstate.

Chapter 9:
The Relief Posties and Problem Solving

We had several relief posties during my eight years at The Post Office, but four of them left a lasting impression on me. Before I introduce them, it is worth explaining some of the challenges a relief postie faces each day. They are often thrown in at the deep end, sorting and delivering a round they have never laid eyes on.

A relief postie, formally known as a Relief Postal Delivery Officer (RPDO), has it tougher than most. They usually do not know the area on the rounds they are assigned to, and I take my hat off to all the relief guys and girls. Their job is often like flying blind. If a postie is unfamiliar with a round, it can make for an incredibly long day.

If I may touch briefly on the good old days of being a relief postie:

It was a whole lot easier to walk into an office when the streets on sorting frames were in alphabetical order as opposed to round order nowadays, for obvious reasons. Anyone could throw a round in by simply following the alphabet; it was basically impossible to fail, or as we say here in Australia, it was *idiot-proof.*

Some delivery rounds have sections that are joined by an alleyway or require a ride around a park to get to the next street, or it can turn out to be nowhere near where you would expect it to be. Unfortunately, that information is usually not given to a relief postie, who simply must do a lot of guessing to find their way to the next delivery point on many occasions.

At times, a relief postie may feel like Bear Grylls finding his way out of a jungle. Yet how much fun is that?!

I recall a delivery round I was assigned to many years back that had so many dead ends and guesses to it that I called into the local bottle shop on the way home and downed an ale in the car park just to relieve the stress before driving home to down quite a few more.

There was a section on that round that I remember vividly, and I still wonder to this day why there wasn't at least a little bit of literature on it in the round file back at the office (where delivery information can be kept and perhaps some hazards and minor issues involving dogs etc. can be documented).

When I first commenced as a postie, I was always told, *keep going left when in doubt*, because that's how delivery rounds generally flowed. However, when I reached the end of a street on that round, I had a feeling that going left would take me back to an area that I had already delivered, so I took a right turn instead.

That idea paid dividends as I took what is commonly known as a dead ride (a ride without delivering any mail), and about 300 metres later I decided that the next right turn should get me to where I needed to go, and it did, well, almost.

The right turn I took was the street before the one I required in my next delivery sequence, but I finally found it and the deliveries recommenced. Everyone talks to themselves at some point of the day, but that little exercise was more like a scene out of the series *Prison Break*, where the main actor kept asking himself where the next tunnel led to for his eventual escape.

Admittedly, I enjoyed my years of being a relief in the postal industry, but some days were more challenging than others. They probably could have been made easier by some posties who perhaps could have either labelled their sorting frame a little better or even offered a bit of literature explaining a few intricacies of their round for the relief postie while they were either on holidays or on sick leave.

I recall once sorting mail on a frame that didn't have one or two streets listed on it because the streets were relatively new and the frame had not been updated with the information, so I took a guess on the delivery sequence (up the odds and down the evens) and the guess paid off.

Problem-solving in the workplace spices up the day, and how boring can the usual ho-hum of everyday work be that at times resembles turning a light switch on at night when you get up for a pee? (Some may find that challenging, but when you think about it, well, most will appreciate what I am saying in that respect anyhow.)

Being a relief postie is challenging yet rewarding, as there are many hurdles to overcome to complete delivery some days. Most posties will only ever experience a couple of days of frustration before it all falls into place, just like finding the last few pieces of a jigsaw puzzle. A relief postie's job is not rocket science; it's common sense with a slight bit of genius thrown in to sort out the finer points of it all.

If nothing else, the relief gig kept the brain active as opposed to doing the same round every day, which most posties can do almost with their eyes closed and without having to think too much about it.

Good fun as a relief postie, never a dull moment.

'Larry'

Now this bloke was on another planet, no other way to describe him. I am uncertain as to whether he wished to make an impression on guys like me who were new to the industry or if that was just his nature, but I likened Larry to that cartoon character, the Tassie Devil.

You have probably seen a clip or two over the years or perhaps remember it from when you were a kid yourself, but the little fella would do something a million miles per hour, sort of like a hurricane going through a paddock. That was Larry through our office.

My first recollection of Larry was him walking into our office and saying g'day to everyone. He usually had a nickname for most guys he knew and if he didn't know them, he would probably ask their name and give them a nickname there and then.

He made it to our post box sorter, a happy-go-lucky Asian gentleman by the name of Hando, who sorted the mail into the post boxes each morning. Calm as you like, Larry came out with this one: "One Hung Low, how are you going today?"

Hando was a ripper bloke and an absolute jet at sorting mail into the post boxes, and we treated him as one of the boys. It took a lot to offend him. Back then, if someone got offended it was usually diffused quickly without a lawsuit attached.

Larry loved impersonating people, and I can still remember him doing one of a lead guitarist that had our boss totally confused. One morning he heard a song on the radio and he got up out of his chair and started doing what guitarists do, complete with the hand movements plus he put his own spin on it.

You've probably noticed it yourself, when a guitarist is really into their music, they close their eyes and slowly move their head up and down, so that's what Larry did, and it was brilliant.

Boss Ted was watching from his office and came over to quiz him about what on earth he was doing. Larry simply explained to Ted that he was having a short break from sorting and stretching his legs while playing a bit of air guitar. I recall Ted just walking off shaking his head because I really don't think he had an answer for that.

Larry upset Phil one morning, who didn't see the funny side of Larry's antics that the rest of us did. I am unsure whether Larry had consumed too much coffee that morning, but he was fairly hyped up. I watched him crawl under the sorting bay to Phil's desk and grab him just above the knee, you know, the old camel bite. Phil literally hit the roof, with his leg unfortunately, and he got out of his chair limping as though he had been hit by a car.

A car named Larry.

Phil called him every name under the sun as he walked gingerly around the office until his leg settled down from the pain of being smashed up against the sorting frame. Larry also owned a distinctive curve on his right index finger which he showed me one day.

A pushbike rider usually held the mail for the next delivery address between the index finger and the middle finger, and it could basically wear the bone down as the index finger would rub on the handlebar. Larry's finger looked deformed as he had been a pushbike postie for most of his life.

Larry also once got the ultimate revenge on a customer who phoned in a complaint about him.

On reaching a delivery point in suburbia, a big German Shepherd greeted him and basically tried to rip Larry's head off. The front gate was wide open as the owner either forgot to shut it or it malfunctioned, as it was one of those huge Hollywood-mansion-type gates that usually open by an electric signal.

Larry managed to get away from the dog without injury but was more pissed off with the complaint that came through from the resident who stated that he 'kicked out' at their dog. Larry explained that it was self-defence as the gate was open, to which the owner disagreed, stating that the gate was closed.

(Seriously? Why would a postie kick out at a dog behind a closed gate??!)

A postie never forgets (sort of like an elephant, as the saying goes) and it wasn't too long until Larry gained the ultimate karma revenge on the customer who told a bit of a fib regarding the gate apparently being closed.

As Larry reached the same address later that week, he spotted the dog running towards him again, but luckily this time the gate was closed. As he started sliding the mail into the letterbox, the dog once again went for Larry, but this time he could only stick his snout through the back of the letterbox; Larry was safe.

The customer's mail, however, wasn't so safe.

As Larry rode off, he watched on (with a slight smirk on his face, he tells me) as the dog proceeded to tear up the mail, perhaps out of frustration that he couldn't tear up Larry, which was obviously his first preference!

Aah yes, karma, a wonderful thing when it goes in your favour.

Funny guy was Larry (still is!) and he made me laugh on more than one occasion. Mad as a cut snake on a well-behaved day, he usually found a way of either upsetting someone or making them laugh. He finally left the postal industry after almost 30 years of service, and I do believe he left his mark on many a post office, and many a postie for that matter.

Loved ya work, Larry.

'Oggy'

Personally, I loved it when Oggy came to our office because he was the king of phrases and always had a brilliant take on just about any topic. He was very descriptive with the names he gave to people he didn't hold in high regard. 'Gormless tit' was his favourite, without question.

Dictionary.com defines *gormless* as stupid, dull or clumsy, so I suppose it is a word that should be used more often in our vocabulary when referring to an imbecile. Yet it rarely is. Oggy was clearly ahead of the rest of us when it came to colourful terminology.

It was possibly one of the most unique phrases I have ever heard in my life.

Oggy was heavily into the AFL and usually on a Monday morning it was time to pull apart most of the matches that were played over the weekend. He usually came out with something that made me laugh; I believe he would have given Roy and HG a run for their money as a 'special comments' type of radio personality.

Oggy delivered his expressions like no other postie I have ever known and he was also rather fond of an acronym or two, and the following story is a classic example of Oggy in full stride:

At one point in his rather long and colourful Oz Post career, Oggy was assigned the temporary role of working as a PDC3, which basically meant he was running the show and wasn't allocated a delivery round. This wasn't at our office but at a neighbouring one a few kilometres down the road.

His daily duties involved redirecting mail, making sure the posties behaved, and taking phone calls from disgruntled customers who may have had their lawn ridden over when it shouldn't have been. Just the basics really, but all necessary parts of running a postal outlet, and someone had to do it.

Eventually, the position became available full time and, to keep management happy, Oggy applied for the role. In his own words, he found the whole idea *rather underwhelming*. At the time the role was advertised, a manager from another outlet brought a starry-eyed applicant into the office and began raving about their qualities as a potential full-time leader.

Oggy wasn't naïve; he could clearly see a classic case of 'teacher's pet syndrome' taking place and he never truly put his heart into the interview. Naturally, the job went to the teacher's pet.

When a role was filled at Oz Post back in the day, management often insisted on a debrief to go over the finer points of why someone didn't get the job. This was when Oggy delivered what may have been the greatest response in Oz Post history.

When the panel asked him about his apparent lack of enthusiasm for the position, Oggy replied, "I came down with a chronic case of NAFAIAISM."

Eyebrows were raised, followed by the obvious question:

"And what does that mean?"

Oggy calmly replied, "It's an acronym. No ambition, f... all interest anyway."

Safe to say, Oggy never applied again for any roles outside his main position at Oz Post, which of course was relief postie. I, along with many others at The Post Office, were more than happy with his decision, and we always enjoyed seeing him when one of our team called in sick with a heart muscle issue.

Absolute pleasure to have worked with you, Oggy. Legend.

'Col'

Now here was a bloke with no highlight reel whatsoever when it came to silly antics, yet he was an essential part of our office. Col was our regular relief postie whenever someone went on holidays or vanished for one reason or another.

Col was the one who first taught me how to ride a motorbike along a footpath without bowling over little old ladies or pedestrians in general. It is one thing to learn how to ride on a road, and a completely different challenge when your bike is loaded with mail and you have to weave in and out of properties from the footpath. You must factor in obstacles such as cars, people, bins and roadworks when delivering mail.

Col was a big unit, probably pushing 100 kilos, and had a demeanour I could only describe as plain, with about as much emotion in his voice as a funeral director, but he knew his stuff. I organised the one on one lesson with him out of frustration because I will never forget the week I upgraded from a pushbike to a motorbike.

Nothing seemed to change in regard to delivery time.

From memory, I went to Postie School a week or two later which sorted some issues out, but Col's tuition in the short term was invaluable.

I was still slow and always the last back on the Honda, just like I had been on the pushbike. Leapy sensed my frustration and sent Col out to teach me the finer points of delivering mail on a motorcycle. One issue I struggled with was the weight of the mail and how the bike should be stacked with product.

I do not recall how many times I dropped the bike that first week, even though I put it on the stand each time I dismounted. It was all about having equal weight on both sides of the pannier bags, which carried a fair bit of weight in letters and magazines. If there was more weight on the stand side of the bike, which was the left, it was pretty clear the bike could topple over, especially if the stand was put down on uneven ground. I learned that more than once.

I also figured out that it was not hard to transfer bundles of mail from one side of the bike to the other. For example, if you had three bundles on the stand side and two on the other, the bike could tip when you put it on the stand due to the weight difference. Little things like that mattered.

I also learned postie etiquette that day with Col.

At one address, I pushed a letter into a letterbox and it shot straight out the back into the garden. Instinctively, I put the stand down, got off the bike and retrieved it. That was when the big fella chimed in and explained how it could have been avoided. He told me to assess the letterbox on the approach, and if I noticed the back was open or the box simply had no back at all, the delivery might need a slight adjustment in technique.

I took that advice from Col as priceless because he was completely right then and still is now. Some letterboxes are about as secure as the Titanic on that fateful night, so a few had to be approached with a bit of caution rather than charging in like a bull to a red flag.

In other words, instead of flicking the mail in and watching it fly out the back, there was another option where it was dropped in with a gentler motion which avoided having to get off the bike to pick it up.

Sizing up certain letterboxes on the approach became second nature and saved a lot of frustration when things were considered properly rather than treating every box the same. Simple things that made future delivery smoother.

There was an art to the job and I was only just learning it. Delivering on the fly was the way to go back then, although the technique changed over the years because some posties forgot to look where they were going and managed to wipe out the odd parked car.

Shit, where did that come from??

Always look up when delivering mail. It can save you a fair bit of grief.

Col also had an obsession that could only be described as a bloke's obsession. Cars, fast cars, Formula 1 cars. He loved them. When our office eventually moved to night sorting to reduce the morning congestion, Col did a few early starts.

I can still picture Col sorting at a frame with a television right next to him that he had dragged from the lunchroom so he could watch a big race while sorting letters. I am not sure what ratio he hit that morning between letters sorted and time spent watching the race, but he met the quota for the morning, so credit to him for initiative. Big gentle giant was Col and he never said a bad word about anyone. He simply did his job and helped us blokes out whenever we wanted a holiday or a day off.

Champion bloke.

Thanks for your input big fella.

The Macedonian Marvel ('Eli')

Eli was another relief who I took a liking to because of his outrageous sense of humour which probably shone through one morning as we sorted mail and listened to the radio. I did not know much about Eli until "Chain Reaction" by John Farnham came on. After that, I knew a whole lot more about him.

It may have been one of the funniest things I had heard regarding a song that was clearly not his favourite. Eli vented his spleen:

"Possibly the worst song I have ever heard in regard to building up a chorus and then repeating it without even a slight change in tone."

Then he sang the chorus himself and I had to admit he was right. I had probably never thought about it that much before.

He kept going:

"Lack of thought and effort. Most choruses at least offer a slight change in tone but this one misses every basic rule. He has built it up then failed miserably to deliver the goods. Not good enough, John."

He explained it all in a way that had me believing the same thing by the end of it. Yep, Chain Reaction was simply not up to scratch.

We all realised we had another livewire relief postie on our hands after that little rant.

Eli had another talent which I am sure he showed us later that same week as he nailed some AFL player impersonations that were uncanny in their likeness.

Eli also had the misfortune of experiencing the full force of Larry's antics one morning when Larry took offence to Eli's choice of shorts. They were long basketball shorts that Eli wore because he could not find his work pair, and Larry made a point of letting him know he did not like them one bit. Eli's pants were pulled down and he was wrestled to the ground.

Looking back, I am surprised Eli volunteered to help us again after being tackled at work by the Tassie Devil himself. I think from that day on, he never wore his basketball shorts again, especially if he knew Larry was in the building.

The Macedonian Marvel can claim to be the only postie I know who single handedly saved a house from a potential fire during his usual relief duties. It must go down in Australia Post history as one of the all time great saves.

When he arrived at a letterbox, he saw smoke coming from a window. He parked the bike, jumped the fence, opened the window using a gardening utensil he found and climbed inside to put out a smoking hotplate. The owner had ducked to the local shops and forgotten to turn it off, which could have ended very badly.

To cut a long story short, the house was saved thanks to Eli's quick thinking and Fireman-like instincts. The owner was extremely grateful. Eli did not need to buy wine for quite some time, as the owner looked after him generously in that respect.

Eli also rivalled my own wildlife-saving effort and probably surpassed it when he helped a family of ducks cross a busy road. One of the ducklings fell down a drain, and Eli retrieved it after borrowing a crowbar from a local tradie who was also there. The family was reunited safely on the other side of the highway.

Is it just me or does this bloke fit the criteria of an all-round Mr Fixit in suburbia?

The final story on Eli's list of postie highlights ended up on National Radio which I heard one morning as they introduced a segment about a local postie who went above and beyond.

A pair of prescription glasses were found on the side of the road by Eli, who took them to a nearby Spec Savers store where they were traced back to the owner through the serial number. A staff member passed the glasses and the story on to the relieved owners, who were so grateful that they phoned the radio station. They interviewed Eli, who described what happened.

There you go, a highlight reel of epic proportions for Eli, a postie who is still delivering in suburbia today some 30 years after the old Post Office days when taking the mickey out of Jonny Farnham's lyrics, wrestling with Larry after being dacked and showing off his AFL impersonations felt like it was only yesterday.

The Macedonian Marvel indeed.

The 'Just a Hand' Customer (*Thing* from The Addams Family)

I have lost count of how many times I have knocked on a customer's door, received no answer, scanned and left a safe drop parcel within arm's length of the front door, usually behind a pot plant or tucked between the front door and the flyscreen. Then, as I have walked away, I have heard the door open, looked back and seen a hand appear, grab the parcel and disappear inside.

Yet not a single word spoken by the customer, just the sound of the door opening and closing. It always reminded me of that famous character from The Addams Family that was only a hand with no body attached.

It was called *Thing*.

I always walked away from those deliveries with a grin, even without a thank you, because my silly mind was already storing ideas for stories like this.

Thing is alive and well on many delivery rounds and adds a bit of spice to being a postie who often receives no accolades yet can still find something to laugh about, especially if they think like I do and categorise customers and deliveries in their own peculiar way.

Chapter 10:
Hiding, Finding, Carding
and Signing for Articles, A Near Miss

The Safe Drop

Here's something that gets a postie's spirits up, a kind gesture by the customer who asked for it or the company that sent the parcel. Drop it safely, gently, no signature needed, no worries, you beauty.

When a parcel falls under that category, it's important to remember the obvious. It should not be visible to everyone, especially if the customer lives opposite a busy road or a school. As an example: "Oh look, a parcel on the front step, fair game, let's take it home and see what's inside."

That's when management become very unhappy with the delivery officer who 'safe dropped' the item.

"Jonny, safe drop mate. Did you realise the customer's front veranda where you left the item in plain sight is opposite a school?"

"Sorry Boss."

Common sense must always come first when safe dropping goods. If you don't have any common sense, then perhaps delivering items is not your ideal way to earn a living. I once saw a parcel with written instructions that stated:

Just throw it over the back fence thanks.

It's up to each postie how they respond to that sort of request, but personally I would look for a safer option that kept the goods out of public view. I even saw a photo once of a parcel placed in a gap in the ceiling of a front veranda. That's stepping into unknown delivery territory.

I always liked the idea of draping a front door mat over a parcel if there was no pot plant available. I never received a complaint about that method. A bin also comes in handy when a veranda is too open to the public, and I was never criticised for bringing an empty bin from the front verge up onto the veranda to hide an item.

I once put a parcel inside a bin, true story.

I delivered to an old beach shack regularly that was always a challenge because there was no sheltered spot for an item on rainy days, due to no overhanging roof eaves.

If the weather was fine, I simply wheeled their bin to the front door and left the item behind it.

One wet day I needed a safe place for a non signature item that wouldn't fit in the letterbox. I checked the green waste bin. It looked like it hadn't seen grass clippings in months, so it didn't stink and seemed like the only practical option. I wheeled the bin to the door, placed the item inside and hoped for the best.

About a week later I met the owner's mum who said:

"Not sure whether it was you, but the postie last week broke new ground with their delivery ideas. My daughter found an item in the green waste bin and was very appreciative."

There you go, sometimes thinking outside the square pays off. If a customer receives a text saying their parcel has been delivered and they come home to find their bin in a different spot, there's a fair chance something is behind it or inside it. If the customer wants the parcel left at their property, then a postie must consider all options, although perhaps not the general waste bin.

I also hid items in electricity meter boxes when they didn't fit in a letterbox, usually on the side of the house. I always left a note in the letterbox explaining where it was because a meter box is hardly the first place a customer checks.

Sometimes a parcel is hidden a little too well, and I have been followed back to my vehicle more times than I can count by customers asking why I knocked on their door.

"Parcel beside the front door Mr Jones, behind the fern pot plant on the left."

It's fascinating. Some people simply forget they ordered anything, so when they hear the doorbell and then see someone walking away, they think someone is playing knock and run. I've had customers step right over their parcel to question me.

At my age, knock and run is not one of my hobbies.

Some companies refuse safe drop options and require signatures only. Fair enough, but some customers get worked up about this 'ignorance' and march down to the delivery centre furious that they asked for a safe drop but didn't get it.

When scanning an item, the postie is simply following the instructions provided which is basically *signature* or *no signature.*

Yet, the postie often gets blamed for 'doing the wrong thing'.

It happens when a customer has requested a *safe drop*, but the company either forgets or ignores the request (which is not the postie's fault).

Sometimes customers and I had informal arrangements for deliveries. Management unfortunately heard about them because occasionally they didn't work out as planned. I once received a call from the boss about one such plan that went pear shaped.

An old school mate asked me to leave his parcel on his balcony as he was getting home late. I couldn't get through the gate to the balcony, so I left it around the back. He thought it was a non signature item, but it wasn't. So I did what any mate would do and signed for it myself, which obviously was not the smartest choice on my part.

When my buddy got home, he didn't look around the back of his house for the item. He had asked me to leave it on his balcony, so he thought it had been stolen when he received the delivery confirmation on his phone.

So off he went to the local postal delivery centre to lodge a complaint, believing his parcel had gone missing. When he returned home, he found the item around the back exactly where I had left it.

Meanwhile, I was being interrogated by the boss after my buddy's complaint came through. I eventually convinced him that it was simply a customer relations issue and that I had only followed instructions.

Then my buddy messaged me:

"Sorry GT, hope I didn't get you into trouble mate. I didn't look around the back. I will call management now and explain the situation."

I replied:

"You fn nob, I was interrogated like a criminal, but I talked my way out of it. You owe me a beer, or three."

He coughed up if my memory serves me right.

Keeping the customer happy is one thing, keeping the company who sent the goods happy is another and keeping management happy is an art on its own. There are many ways to look at it, but if I could offer some advice for new posties in particular, it would be this:

NEVER sign for a customer's item even if he is your best mate. A favour for a buddy can go pear shaped.

NEVER open a side gate if there is even a slight chance a dog lives there. It can get ugly.

IF you can't hide a non-signature item safely out the front of a property and you don't wish to go around the back for fear of meeting a dog, the equation is simple, card it, but also explain briefly as to why you carded it.

DON'T hide the parcel TOO well, you may get tackled by a customer while you are walking back to your vehicle as they may think you are just playing a game with them.

PLEASE don't blame the postie if you requested your parcel to be safely left at your premises and it wasn't adhered to; it probably had more to do with the company who you ordered the item from who didn't honour your request.

The Card

Most posties have experienced frustration with the carding system when a customer does not answer the door. Management used to tell us to knock three times on arrival.

I always followed the rule. Knock, knock, knock.

If nobody answered within a reasonable time, I would start filling out the card. Sometimes I knocked again while writing, just in case they had not heard me the first time.

Personally, I was never a fan of the long foreign surnames such as 'Papadopolous' as they take forever to write. Add a long surname to a potential 15 to 20 digit tracking code and you have the number one pet hate of a postie; the carding process.

So, to the process and how it can often play out:

It all starts with the card, obviously (Sorry We Missed You), writing the surname, the date, the time, the code on the item, what time the customer can pick the item up, placing the card in the door or under the door, taking a photo of the card on the scanner to prove you made an effort as the delivery officer and the job is complete (well, almost.)

As you are on your way out of the driveway, the door then opens.

"YOOHOO MR POSTIE, I AM HOME!!!"

A customer once came to the door after I had completed the carding process and she said the following to me, "Sorry, I was on the phone. I heard you knock. I was doing my best to get to the door."

'Doing her best', while on the phone.... Yep, that's what she said.

As for reactions, it usually comes down to three options:

Option 1: "Oh, you are home!"

Option 2: "You are fn kidding me." (Said quietly or under your breath.)

Option 3: "It is alright, just give me a moment while I reverse the process."

Personally I chose Option 2 more than anything else.

The Near Miss

Personally, I never had a serious accident on either a pushbike or motorbike, unless you count dropping the bike, which is more stupidity than anything else. Maybe I was just lucky, because I had some close calls.

Slow posties tend to avoid accidents and I was always reasonably cautious. I never really liked motorbikes. As a kid I fell off a little motorbike and burned my leg on the exhaust. I don't think I touched a motorbike again until I graduated from pushbike duties.

Some posties had frequent falls, nothing major. Unless the bike was damaged, most would not even mention it.

I once heard about a postie's motorcycle throttle becoming stuck, so he had to slide out on a grass verge and ended up being wedged underneath a car.

Sounded a bit stressful to say the least.

A dangerous job at times it can be as avoiding motorists who simply don't see you is a daily occurrence for a postie that creates a bit of stress here and there, so looking ahead and thinking FOR drivers is a necessity for a postie. Roundabouts on a postie bike are never a dull moment. Some posties have been wiped out by motorists who usually came out with the same statement:

Sorry, I didn't see the bike.

It is not that hard to see a motorbike unless your eyes are painted on. These days postie bikes have flags to help motorists spot them.

About ten years ago, I had one of the strangest near misses of my life. My round was a few kilometres out of town and allowed speeds up to 80, although I preferred 60 to 70 to be safe.

As I reached my first delivery point, I threw the mail into the letterbox then hit a slight bump as the terrain was somewhat rough. The bike suddenly stopped, and I had to dismount in a hurry to avoid falling off.

As I picked the motorbike up, I looked it over and saw that the back wheel had moved to the left and become jammed up against the frame.

Knowing nothing about motorbike mechanics, I simply knew I wasn't going anywhere, anytime soon. I began calling the boss for a replacement bike when the guy next door started reversing out of his driveway. I had a quick chat with him, explained the situation and he gave me a lift back to the office after we took the bike around the side of the house and obviously, I took the mailbags with me.

I collected another bike, finished the round and the boss went out to retrieve the bike in question with the help of another postie.

Turns out a rear wheel nut had been left off the day before when a mechanic changed the tyre. It was pure luck that it didn't come loose while I was doing 70 on the way out.

The mechanic admitted the mistake and life went on. These days posties do a bike check each morning and it makes sense. I am sure I did mine back then too, but I clearly missed the missing nut.

Pays to look over the bike properly. Trust me.

The 'Walk alongside your Postie' Customer

Wal, a retired postie and former team leader with around forty years of Oz Post service behind him, once told me about a customer who relied on the postie for his daily dose of mental stimulation. The bloke would wait at his front gate every single day for Wal to arrive, then walk the entire way around the cul de sac with him while he delivered the mail, sometimes even breaking into a little jog to keep up.

His commitment could not be questioned.

He was determined to get the absolute maximum out of his postie to help soothe his troubled mind and if that meant chasing Wal around the street while mail was being delivered, then that is what he would do.

It is completely your choice if you want to follow your postie around while they work, but it is probably not practical and would get tiring very quickly. Perhaps invite them over for a beer after work instead. That might work a little better.

Chapter 11:
More Legends of The Post Office
and The Tweak

Kel

As mentioned earlier in The Radio post, Kel had a sharp wit and, paired with a fairly strong English accent, his humour was even more entertaining. A bit like the Aussie Irish comedian Jimeoin, who could say he was popping down to the local supermarket and it would sound funny simply because of the way he said it.

Kel had picked up the title of WA Postman of the Year a couple of years before I arrived at The Post Office, so he clearly knew the job inside out, on top of being a funny bugger. He produced a story or two on a regular basis and one of them involved the postie's greatest nemesis, the dog.

His run in with a small dog had me in stitches because the way he described it was priceless. Kel told us about a day from hell where he was dealing with heavy rain, junk mail and generally having a pretty miserable time on the bike, when he was confronted by a yapping dog.

The dog was a type of jack russell that bailed him up outside a property while he was trying to shove letters and junk mail into a letterbox. The dog refused to leave him alone, almost blocking him from getting to the box, so Kel eventually snapped.

He leaned down, picked the dog up and threw it straight over the fence. Kel insisted the fence was not very high and he did not hear the dog yelp or anything. It hit the ground running with its tail between its legs.

I still picture that story whenever I see a dog suffering from small animal syndrome and wonder what it would be like to repeat that particular incident. We all respond differently to certain situations, but throwing an annoying animal over a fence just to get some peace probably takes the cake.

Kel always entertained during primary sorting where his wit could knock you down in an instant. I will never forget what I still believe is the greatest comeback to typical male banter I have ever heard.

I clearly remember one bloke bragging about the length of his old fella, probably Chris, when Kel fired back with a pearler:

"Ten inches? Lucky you, wish I had ten inches instead of this big awkward thing."

Laugh?

The entire office lost it. Kel could flatten you with ease no matter what you said because he always had a reply that made your comment sound ordinary.

Many thanks Kel for entertaining us over the years at The Post Office. Champion.

Pardo

I am still unsure how to describe the guy we welcomed as a new recruit around 1998. Pardo received a guernsey with us and at first I thought he was a walking statue. He barely said a word, just "g'day" and a few comments here and there. It was as though he came from another country and had no idea how to hold a conversation.

For some odd reason, I was given the job of taking him out and showing him a delivery round, which to this day remains one of the most entertaining days of mail delivery I have ever seen.

Pardo arrived with glowing reports about his postie expertise and I am still not sure where he actually came from, apart from possibly another planet. One thing remains true to this day when someone shows up with all the bells and whistles:

They were not welcome back where they came from.

"Yep, he is a superstar, we are so sorry to see him go, he will be sorely missed."

"Bullshit. He was useless and you cannot wait to see the back of him."

Always look closely at character references. The ones without all the bells and whistles are the ones you want, not the supposed 'superstars'.

On Pardo's first day, I loaded his bike and followed behind, waiting to be dazzled by the brilliance mentioned in his resume. It took maybe two deliveries to see the truth. Pardo was an absolute superstar of the Honda 110, no doubt at all, but he lacked one important thing about being a postie: putting the mail in the letterbox.

Some letterboxes are more difficult to deliver to than others, as I have stated before, but Pardo was so keen to impress that he simply wedged the corner of each letter as close as he could to the slot and then took off. I spent nearly three hours tidying up his mess that I can only describe as mayhem. He basically completed the entire run on the fly.

Some deliveries fell straight onto the ground after he rode off, but he was not looking back to check his work. Stopping for any reason was not on Pardo's schedule that day.

That afternoon when we returned to the office, Team Leader Leapy asked:

"How'd he go?"

"Yep, quick, really quick, seems to know his stuff on the bike."

I didn't know what else to say.

The bloke who taught me how to deliver, Col, explained that it is essential to never leave mail hanging out of a letterbox, yet I had just witnessed three hours of chaos and the best I could come up with was that he was quick.

I was not about to tell anyone that Pardo was the complete opposite of a postie. He was like a graffiti artist who relied on someone else cleaning up after him. He would get better, surely, if only he slowed down, and I think he eventually did. At one point Chris had a go at him for being a slack arse, which went down about as well as a fart in an elevator.

Looking back, Pardo was an all or nothing type of postie. He either moved at the speed of sound or the speed of a sloth when he wanted over-time. If he had found a middle ground he might have been a decent delivery officer.

He once told me he ran over a dog and apologised to the owner, explaining he was in a hurry and couldn't stop. It did not surprise me but I still don't know if the story was true. Normally if a postie hit a dog, the whole office would hear about it.

Both Carlos and Chris threatened to kill him at least once because they didn't see eye to eye on certain parts of the job, but that only added to the fun at The Post Office. Some personalities simply don't gel and Pardo had a knack of annoying more than one fellow postie. Personally, I didn't mind him too much, provided he did not speak, because when he did he usually offended someone.

Pardo eventually left the postal industry several years later to take up a job in the woodworking trade.

Hopefully for everyone's sake, he turned his wood a bit slower than he used to turn his postie bike.

'Thorney'

This bloke was usually as busy as the proverbial one-armed bricklayer in Baghdad because he had two jobs, one as a postie and the other as a painter. I would witness Thorney on many occasions roll back into the office carpark after he had completed his delivery round, then walk out ten minutes later dressed as a painter, complete with paint-spattered clothes.

(I suppose that's how a painter dresses.)

Right from the start of my tenure, Thorney liked having a shot at my supposed lack of work ethic because I was usually the last postie back, so he assumed I was hanging, or as Thorney would say in his strong English accent, 'anging.

That is a terminology used at most postal outlets when someone is last back and perhaps hanging out for some overtime and a meal allowance. So on most days, Thorney would read the hours book in the morning to see when the other guys finished their rounds the previous day, and usually he would slip into me:

"You 'anging ey GT?"

"Ang, ang, anga you are," with that strong accent and he always left the h off the beginning of the word.

I beat him back on delivery once on a rainy day when I saw storm clouds rolling in and I did not have my wet-weather jacket with me, so I put the foot down and tore through my last half of delivery and got him by a whisker, which he acknowledged:

"Cannot believe it, I have been a postie for 15 years and some new kid comes in and beats me back."

I think that was fairly standard with the older guys who had been in the game for years; it was a pride thing not to be shown up by a new bloke. Most days would be somewhat of a race to see who could get their mail sorted first and delivered.

They left Carlos alone from day one however, as he was basically a freak show with his sorting and delivery speed, and he could show anyone up even if he did not know the round too well. Some guys just had a knack for sorting and delivering mail quickly, whereas others were a bit slower and took their time (like me.)

Quite ironically, Thorney ended up on my round one January due to a round change where we played musical posties and moved one spot along in the office so a new delivery run could be learned. Great idea in my mind, as it was invaluable for the office to have guys know more than one delivery run for obvious reasons.

Anyhow, to cut a long story short, Thorney came back LAST on the day I set my round up for him and he walked in like a bloke who had just run a marathon.

"Shit that's a big run you got there GT."

"Aint mine anymore Thorney, it's yours now champ!"

(I had waited possibly two years to say that to him.)

I don't believe I received any more flak from him after that, as I think he felt bad that he had given me the shits for so long about coming back last. I was not the fastest postie there, but I knew I had a reasonable-sized round, so it was an exercise in patience looking back on it, as I knew I wasn't going to be the last back forever.

From memory, I believe Thorney took that mantle from me with great regularity over the following year as I was put onto a round that took me a bit less time. It was impossible to make all rounds even, as some had the kilometres but not the mail volume, whereas others had the opposite. It was luck of the draw.

Haven't seen Thorney in 30 years, but I have heard a whisper that he is out there somewhere with a paintbrush doing what he used to do after delivering his postie round way back in the 90s.

I sincerely hope you are doing a great job and not 'anging Thorney...

'Burns'

The biggest highlight reel of The Post Office (aside from Larry and Kurt) was Burns, but mainly for all the wrong reasons. He was the slowest on delivery, the most inaccurate primary sorter and probably owned the longest complaints file in the office for delivery indiscretions.

But boy, he was funny.

He had a mind that could change song lyrics as soon as a tune came on the radio, which requires a fair bit of skill. Remember Foreigner's classic? "You're as cold as ice, willing to sacrifice..." Burns one day came out with his own version: "You're as small as mice, willing to squeak through life."

That is talent from any angle.

Burns and Kurt were as thick as thieves and they would often sing a duet together. They regularly rolled out a Captain Sensible masterpiece by the name of 'Wot'. Anyone from my era would know this song from the 70s, an absolute classic (I said Captain, I said what, or rather, wot.)

They would take turns singing the chorus which was, in a word, terrible, but great fun regardless.

Burns was the most inaccurate mail sorter and it was proven by the occasional sorting test where all our primary sorted product had to be initialled before handing it over, so we could see who the culprit was as far as mis-sorts were concerned. Burns won hands down every time, and even though we did our best to tell him what mistakes he was making, it was assured that on the very next test, the very same mistakes would be made.

I loved the fact that Burns was the type of bloke you could convince easily. One Friday morning the phone rang at around 5.55 am and we just knew that it would be someone wanting a long weekend.

I answered the call.

"Burns?"

"Yep."

"What is wrong with ya?"

"I am sick."

(I was far from convinced, so I challenged him ever so politely.)

"No you're not, it is Friday and you want a long weekend, as we all do. Come in buddy. If you're a bit under the weather, we'll help you deliver the run."

Burns turned up 15 minutes later and we helped him deliver his round after he had sorted it, as sorting was the most time consuming part, not the delivery, particularly if most of the posties took around 15 minutes worth of delivery. It is commonly known as a split, where a delivery round is shared among fellow workmates.

One day he told us he was having a day off the following week to move house, which management allowed back then.

I vividly recall saying to him, "So you want a day off to move a sports bag full of clothes Burns? You don't own anything!"

I think with Burns you sometimes had to spell things out to him and he eventually got it. I was not a bully; I just knew Burns needed a bit of perspective now and then. Burns was always paid more than the rest of us because he was never really in a hurry.

It was as though he was simply enjoying the great outdoors in his chosen profession and was not interested in deadlines or time targets. Now, it was not as if you could spend all day out there; you had to at least make an effort to deliver the mail within a certain timeframe, so most of us would go pretty hard, but not Burns.

He was his own boss, where nothing and no one could take him out of his comfort zone. Chris tried one day while he was team leader, but it was like talking to a brick wall, despite a raised voice and hand gestures trying to explain that the job was not supposed to pay for a skiing holiday in Aspen through overtime.

Burns was brilliant, possibly the most well liked postie at The Post Office because nothing phased him. Chris's effort with him was like watching a bloke at a pub try to assert his authority and the guy he was talking to responding with something like, 'Yeah ok mate, I am just going for another drink, what you having?'

Carlos once caught Burns on his way out of The Post Office carpark on his Honda 110 not wearing his helmet. Burns wondered what all the yelling was about.

"You forget something Burns?"

"Aah shit, that was lucky, I was wondering why the bike sounded a bit louder today."

(True story.)

Haven't seen Burns in 20 something years.

If you get a copy of this book buddy, I miss ya!

The Boss (Ted)

Ted was definitely no highlight reel like some of his postie employees but a really nice bloke. He gave me a start in '93, and I am forever indebted to him.

Ted was about 5 foot nothing and was not exactly what you would call an intimidating figure, however he was patient and that is exactly what was required when looking after a team of posties who at times resembled a naughty bunch of schoolboys testing the boundaries.

It was Ted who I spoke to on that day in '93 when I simply asked if I could help out with some deliveries at Christmas time, and it was Ted who had the final say. Well, perhaps he ran it by Team Leader Leapy as well, but ultimately it was Ted who placed me on my first Oz Post payroll.

I was probably not his worst employee in my first two to three months at The Post Office, though Ted did give me some leeway without a doubt. During that time frame, which ultimately became my probation period, I limped into work with that well described foot injury, yet he still allowed me to deliver. He also showed me some compassion when I spewed up the contents of a previous night's beer drinking binge.

I can safely say that my probation period was not entirely smooth, but I turned up regardless of my condition, so I suppose Ted gave me some slack in that respect.

As explained, Kurt had no filter and one day he got wind of the fact that Ted had a bad haemorrhoid condition, which looking back on, was probably a condition you really did not want Kurt to know about.

We were down a staff member through sickness one day during Ted's rather nasty condition and Kurt, in front of the whole office, came out with the following:

"Hey Ted, what about jumping on a pushbike and coming out to help us do that extra round? We will find you a bike with an extra soft seat!"

I don't remember what Ted's answer was, however I don't think he was in any condition to jump on a pushbike, and I don't believe Kurt was on Ted's Christmas card list after that either. Kurt pushed the boundaries more than most and no one was safe, including the boss.

Ted, if you ever read this book, you gave me a start in what became a 23 year career in Oz Post, so if you look back on your past judgement of potential and eventual employees, well, I may have had a rough initiation period but I smoothed out the early deficiencies and became a reasonable postie.

Hope you are enjoying your retirement.

The 'Tweak'

I was once asked by a customer, "So do you ever get bored delivering the same round each day?"

"How long have you got?" I replied.

I then proceeded to explain the tweak of the postal system, which took a while to do, and if my memory serves me correctly, any future questions from that customer about my job were limited to, "So, how is this weather for delivering mail hey?"

Owning a mind that I can only describe as *overactive* can at times be an issue, particularly if you are a postie.

Tweaking a delivery round is a way to help a postie take away some of the boredom or the same old routine. It is a test of the mind, similar to how a fitness fanatic changes up their routine from one day to another to avoid complacency.

I believe the main reason I wanted to take on the position of an RPDO, Relief Postie or Relief Postal Delivery Officer, at my second office on the south coast, was because I loved the idea of variety. I have heard of some posties delivering the same round for ten years or more and while that idea has merit for reducing the possibility of delivery mistakes when a new postie takes over, the idea bored me senseless.

One of the most challenging delivery rounds I had ever been assigned to was a business district round done on foot with a trolley. It covered perhaps a couple of hundred businesses at a guess, maybe more, plus a few kilometres. Initially I looked at the entire round as something too long on foot and in need of a change to save some leg work.

I did not mind the exercise, but I felt it could be done more as a fifty-fifty delivery, half walking and half bike, just for the sake of it. My thinking was this: I was on that round for a month while someone was on holidays and I had to spice it up, so that is exactly what I did.

After around a week or so of sizing the whole thing up, the tweak was in full swing.

I would take the trolley first thing in the morning after sorting was completed and deliver shopping centres and areas that were too difficult to access by bike. On average it took around an hour or so of brisk walking, maybe a bit more on a busy day.

I would then usually run back to the delivery centre with a pie and a drink that I bought from the last business I delivered to, a bakery that I strategically worked into the last section of the round. After inhaling the pie, which used to go down quickly after an early morning power walk, I opted for the motorcycle to service the less busy areas.

Admittedly, there was quite a bit of parking involved and walking the mail into shops because I did not want to stray too far from the bike, for obvious reasons, but the new system worked beautifully.

Without boring you with all the details, I changed a delivery round that took anywhere between two and three hours of walking, depending on how busy it was, and turned it into an even spread of walking and bike delivery.

A complete tweak.

At a guess, I would say I saved around an hour of walking each day on that round, and I once ran the entire walking section because I had an appointment to make and finished it in 45 minutes.

The old postal trolleys were easy to run with back then. I would not even attempt it nowadays as the new high-tech delivery trolleys could double as ice cream vending machines, and trying to run with one might offer some complications.

Sometimes a tweak gives a time advantage, but in most cases it simply gives a postie a different view of a delivery round and tests their creativity at the same time. I was forever changing motorcycle delivery rounds because after a couple of days I could usually see a better way of doing the delivery or I simply became bored with the same routine.

The Bill Murray classic "Groundhog Day" can definitely be associated with mail delivery if a postie never changes things up when they are assigned to a round for any length of time. I vividly recall some days taking sections of mail that were last on the sorting frame and delivering them at the start of the round.

I suppose it is fair to say my delivery methods were not conventional a lot of the time, and luckily I never had an accident, as I may have copped some grief the next day if another postie took over my round and was not in sync with my tweaking.

Delivery rounds can be set up in many ways, but the blueprint on the sorting frame has been deemed the most efficient. It is up to the individual postie to change it.

So, did I ever mess up a tweak?

Most were reasonably smooth with the occasional thought of, *Where the heck am I and how do I get back to where I need to be to finish this round?* Looking back, I suppose I can honestly say that I always found my way back to the office after a tweak.

Read into that what you will.

The 'Allow your Dogs to keep Barking' Customer

On one of my regular parcel deliveries, I always used to park the van at the top of a steep driveway and as soon as I stepped out, the two dogs living there started barking. I used to cringe whenever I saw a parcel for that address because the dogs were not big but very aggressive.

Getting the parcels through the gate was always an issue.

If I put my stopwatch on from the moment I parked the van and located the parcels from the back, to the time I placed the parcels on the ground at the customer's side gate and scanned them, I would say it took about two minutes.

Two minutes of constant barking. I am no dog expert, but most customers are usually up and about quickly if they hear their dogs going off.

Not so with these guys.

After placing two smaller parcels into a large letterbox, I tried to get the big parcel through the gate, but the two dogs would not allow it because they were determined to stop me entering the property. I knew the owners were home because I saw the back door wide open and two cars in the driveway.

Call it postie intuition if you like.

So, it was then that I lost my patience and had a few words with the dogs in question:

"GET OUT OF IT!!"

A big fella then ran out of the back door as though his house was on fire and rushed towards me as if I had attacked his pets. (Hey, I did not physically touch either of them, I simply yelled at them.)

"WHAT ARE YOU DOING YELLING AT MY DOGS??"

"Mate, I am trying to deliver you a parcel and your dogs are trying to eat me in the process!"

He came back with, "Well, that does not give you the right to yell at my dogs!"

I thought that was an interesting answer from a dog owner.

I walked off shaking my head and it occurred to me that this type of customer is happy for their dogs to bark constantly without even checking why they are barking. Yet when someone *barks* back, that's when the customer's ears finally prick up.

If you are one of these customers, please put yourself in the shoes of a postie who is simply trying to deliver your items and don't turn it into something that resembles a warzone that he or she has to endure just to get the items to your front door.

If a customer asked for their item to be left without a signature, then I would do everything possible to leave it. On some occasions, the parcel would have to be carded and taken back to the postal outlet due to circumstances preventing delivery, despite the obvious risk of upsetting the customer.

If your dogs are going off, there is probably a valid reason, particularly if you have done some online shopping recently. Your postie may have just arrived, so please roll out the welcome mat and maybe put the dogs away.

Just a suggestion.

Chapter 12:
Lost Items, School Visits, Funny Names and Flyday

Lost Coffee

If I were to explain one of my biggest stuff ups while delivering mail or parcels, it would be the following story. (I also believe that Specsavers could look at making a new television ad involving a postie, a parcel and a happy ending.)

After arriving home nice and early one lunchtime from a relatively quiet day on parcel delivery, I received a phone call from my boss:

"GT, we have a query on a parcel that you apparently dropped at a customer's doorstep last week, but they say they have not received it."

Whenever you receive a call like that, you immediately become suspicious of the customer's agenda because there is no way in the world that a postie could have made an error. Yeah right, dream on.

Modern technology however is a wonderful thing because it finds mistakes and shows that some people do make errors even though they would rather believe otherwise. I asked the boss if he would mind sending me a photo of the safe drop because that would shed some light on where I left the parcel.

After studying the photo, I vividly remember telling myself in no uncertain terms:

Yep, you are an idiot GT.

At the first glance, I knew that the parcel's correct destination was not the one I had photographed.

If I have not already explained, the latest scanners in the postal industry allow a postie to take a photo of where they leave a parcel, so if it goes missing it is easier to trace. In this case, it was obvious straight away that it was not where I should have delivered it because the front doorstep should have been wooden, not brick paved.

Ah, modern tech, love it.

I drove around to the customer's house and we had a long conversation as we both tried to work out where on earth the parcel had been delivered the week before. And before we go too far, it was $245 worth of coffee, not a $5 tee-shirt.

My theory was this: I delivered it to the wrong street, but perhaps the correct number, or maybe even the wrong number but the correct street. As I have already written elsewhere in this book, it happens either through mis-sorting, stupidity or a mix of both.

I told the customer, a lovely lady, that I would take a drive, retrace some steps and be back with an answer in no time, and that is exactly what I did. It took less than ten minutes to find the mistake. The customer's house number, for the sake of this book, where the coffee should have been delivered was number 55. However, I delivered the parcel to number 15. Correct street, incorrect number.

When I drove past number 15, it all came back to me. I remembered driving up their rather steep driveway and dropping the parcel on the doorstep, a paved doorstep, and taking a photo of it for proof of delivery.

So, I knocked on their door and hoped they were home. And unlike another instance I had experienced, where a customer denied receiving an incorrectly addressed item, I also prayed they still had the $245 worth of coffee.

Unfortunately, they were not home, but the neighbour heard me knocking, came around and told me that the owners only came to town twice a week, yet he had their mobile number.

He made a phone call:

"Jim, the postie is at your house, made a mistake last week. Do you have his parcel?"

Jim replied, "Yeah sure do, it is inside, I will be in town in two days."

Brilliant.

I drove back to number 55 and spoke to Mrs Jones:

"Found the coffee Mrs Jones, I will get it to you by Friday, trust me."

I messaged the hierarchy:

All sorted Boss, found the coffee. Long story but she will have it by Friday.

For the record, Mrs Jones received her $245 worth of coffee, management didn't have to compensate her and the neighbour who saved the day received a six pack of beer from me, plus, the postie kept their reputation intact, well sort of.

I even gave Mrs Jones a free copy of this book.

Don't you just love a happy ending?

School Visits

I was once asked by my boss if I would mind talking to a bunch of primary school kids and telling them what a postie does.

I thought, *Sure, why not? How hard could that be?*

So off I went to a primary school or two, talked about my life as a postie and answered the usual questions.

"So how many times have you been bitten by a dog?"

"Have you ever fallen off your bike?"

At least most of them paid attention to who I was and what my job involved, so I did not have to answer the same question as that poor bloke in the Hilux ad, "What do you do again?"

"I drive a Hilux."

Come on, everyone has seen that ad surely.

It was pretty obvious what I did from the moment I walked through the classroom door with my helmet on and a bundle of letters in my hand. Being a postie is one of those jobs that is fairly simple to understand, although one kid was completely uninterested.

He put his hand up and told me what his own dad did for a job because he was not interested in mine. Fair enough, being a postie is not everyone's cup of tea.

Once I had the school visits down to an art, I was then asked to talk to some kids who came to the local post office on excursions. That was hilarious due mainly to the peanut gallery in the background. I would often hear a laugh or two from Wal and the Boss in their office or the occasional comment after I had said something to the kids that they thought could have been phrased better.

Initially, I found the whole thing somewhat daunting; throwing mail into a frame and trying to do it at lightning speed to impress them but once I started receiving positive feedback, it made it all worthwhile.

"Wow, look at how fast he sorts!"

When I heard that a few times, it made me feel like the bloke in the Hilux ad when his daughter smiles at him as if to say, "Onya Dad". My two youngest kids were part of those visits, so I had to get it right because the pressure was on.

After showing the class how to throw a letter into a sorting frame, we moved out into the bike shed. I would load up the bike and ask the usual questions:

"So, what happens if I don't distribute the mail evenly onto both sides of the bike?"

Or:

"Who can tell me what these things are and why I take them with me when delivering the mail?"

(I would then hold up a packet of dog biscuits and that usually got a reaction, from the teachers as well.)

You would then hope that the bike started on the first attempt, otherwise the whole class would laugh at you, teachers included. A bit of pressure being the demonstrator at your local mail distribution centre because, let's face it, you didn't want to look like a clown in front of that many kids and their teachers, and I definitely didn't want my own kids disowning me.

"Is that your Dad? He is a bit of a goose."

"Nope, never seen him before."

Thanks Wal and Boss, the peanut gallery, for the special comments in the background during those school visits. I notice you two were nowhere to be found when they were looking for someone to fly the flag for the postal industry.

Funny Names, Literature and the occasional Rabbit

Every postie has delivered goods to a customer with a funny name and sometimes it is hard to keep a straight face when you are standing in front of one, especially when asking for a signature.

I had one gentleman who, rather than say his surname out loud, spelt it instead because he worked in a retail store and was cautious about anyone overhearing it. I honestly cannot remember the name apart from the fact that it resembled a porn star's stage name, but I can tell you this, it rivalled Callum Murray from that humorous drink advertisement on television.

Some kids are dealt a cruel blow in life, and it can start very early on if their parents aren't careful with their choice of names. However, in most cases, it's not their fault as surnames are obviously passed down from one generation to the next.

One name I can share is *Lurgey McSandwich*, as I know for a fact that was not the gentleman's real name at that address. I believe he had simply had a few beers while online shopping one night and decided to try his luck with the company he was ordering from, who obviously did not ask for identification.

I have delivered to *John Smith* and I did ask the obvious question:

"So, Mr Smith, I hope you do not mind me asking, but is this really your name?"

He was a fairly cheerful bloke, so I trusted my judgement in asking, because I was never going to let that one go without questioning Australia's most common male name. Never question an aggressive customer's name as you may end up in trouble.

I once went into a business and asked the lady at the front counter if I could please see *Jack Littlewilly*, as that was the name on the parcel. She burst out laughing and called the whole office to see if anyone knew a *Mr Littlewilly*. A young bloke stepped forward; he had simply ordered under a different name, as you do.

I have seen a parcel addressed to *One Hung Low*, which for some reason I did not believe was genuine. Some customer names over the years can brighten your day, whether they are real or not.

Always be cautious when asking about a customer's name because it can mean the difference between getting abused or sharing a laugh. I am no human nature expert, but I believe I am a reasonable judge of character, and I never once got belted for asking the wrong question about a name.

Just lucky, I guess.

Some writing on the front and back of letters and parcels defies common sense, and I have seen some that were priceless. One of my favourites was a letter returned to sender by an ex-girlfriend or partner, possibly even an ex-wife:

Doesn't live here anymore, kicked him out, his penis kept falling into other women.

True story.

I sorted a parcel one morning with the return address *Glenthompson 3293* (a town in Victoria). Now, how many people have a town named after them, hey?

The Dead Rabbit

The red drop boxes around suburbia where customers post items each day for collection can produce some interesting surprises for postal staff. At Xmas time a few years back, I heard a scream from a female staff member and rushed from the delivery shed to the retail area to see what had happened.

Nothing serious.

Someone had posted a dead rabbit which ended up on the sorting bench when one of the mail bags was emptied. Understandably, it scared the hell out of the staff member. There was no point in taking it to the local vet though; it was long gone.

Anything can happen some days in the world of post, and the unpredictability keeps the job interesting. Go on, when was the last time you saw a dead rabbit appear on your bench at work?

Friday (*Flyday*)

There's probably not a postie alive who hasn't looked back on a big day of delivery and thought to themselves, *How f....n good am I?!* (or words to that effect.)

Personally, some days after a huge volume of deliveries, I was looking for a ticker tape parade on my way out of the distribution centre to applaud my efforts. Most performances, however, went unnoticed by everyone except me.

Probably most jobs, let's be honest.

Most fellow posties would agree because as long as the round is completed each day, everyone is happy, especially management, although many do not see the skill involved in some of the methods used to get the job done.

Some days looked like an impossibility to finish because of the hours available compared with the volume presented because it's not as though as a postie you have all day and night to deliver the product.

The Belinda Carlisle song from 1989, "Leave a Light on For Me", should never be taken literally by a postie. The Post Office in the 90s operated much the same as today; they had to close at some point, usually at 5 pm or 5.30 pm during Christmas.

Retail staff locked the doors, and it was up to the posties to return before closing, whether the mail was delivered or not.

Sometimes it simply was not possible to deliver everything, and there was an art to predicting how much volume to take out each day.

The four day break over Easter was usually the toughest because the mail kept coming in and building up until the posties caught up.

I vividly remember one of my first delivery days on a push bike, returning late to the office and being politely told by a retail staff member that they did have a life outside of Oz Post and were looking forward to getting home for dinner.

I got the hint; it did not happen again.

So, to Friday or *Flyday* as it is still called.

It is a day where most posties in Australia find an extra gear, literally, because it offers a long weekend of sorts. Back in the 90s I basically had a job where I worked four and a half days a week because most Fridays I finished between 12 and 1 pm.

Mail volume tapered off after a heavy start to the week, and Friday was generally a doddle where some record delivery times were set. On one particular Friday I delivered my last item by 10 am because I was heading away for a long weekend, so I started sorting at about 4.30 am, smashed the sorting, and then completed a Moto Grand Prix style bike run.

The rules back then were different from today, where a 4.30 am start nowadays for a postie is basically impossible due to the fact that the product is not usually available for sorting by that hour. There was always something more important on a Friday than work, and we usually found a way to earn a two and a half day weekend.

Yes indeed, *Flyday* was a day all of us posties back in the good old days looked forward to, and it often became a friendly competition to see who could get back the earliest. My good mate Carlos usually took the gold each week; everyone else was happy with bronze or silver.

So, does *Flyday* still exist?

If your postie delivers something around lunchtime on a Friday and your house is at the end of their round, there is a good chance *Flyday* is still alive and the postie has a two and a half day weekend coming up.

But please, don't jump to any conclusions about their speed, because traditionally, by Friday the volume of product has dropped to such an extent that it's usually a half-day-doddle anyhow.

The 'Generous' Customer

I have met a few over the years, particularly around Christmas time when the holidays begin and spirits are usually high. I used to return to the office in December with gifts from appreciative customers. These gifts seemed to dwindle over the years, but in the early days of delivery during the 1990s, it was commonplace to receive a beer or two from more than one happy soul in suburbia. I once received a whole carton of beer, which was a challenge to fit onto the Honda, but a welcome one.

I have been offered an ale on more than one occasion over the festive season while out delivering, but had to decline for obvious reasons.

My most cherished customer was an elderly lady who would meet me at the front gate, usually twice a week, to hand me a slice of cake and a glass of cordial. I seemed to make her day with my mail deliveries.

As I have already explained in this book, I felt appreciated right from the start of my postal career when an elderly gentleman met me at his front gate and handed me ten bucks.

At the time, I was simply filling in on that round and should have given it to the postie who had done the round all year, however if my memory serves me correctly, I was broke at the time and the ten dollars was going to keep me alive until that first payday.

Later in my career, during van deliveries, I found that wine-ordering customers were the most generous, particularly if I carried a few boxes up a flight of stairs into their house. I lost count of how many gave me a sample of their products, which I always dropped around to my mum and dad on the way home because I don't drink wine, just beer. Yet I appreciated the gesture regardless.

If you are a generous customer, keep it up. The world needs more people like you.

Chapter 13:
In Memory Of... and The Reunion

Three of the seventeen posties who 'graced' the floors and sorting frames of The Post Office are no longer with us, yet I have fond memories of all three. They were fantastic blokes, each with either a unique sense of humour or a drama-free way of going about their daily business while sorting or delivering mail, unlike some of the other larrikins I have written about in this book.

Nothing I write here can truly do justice to their personalities or their work ethic for Oz Post, but I will do my best to capture their individual traits. They left an impression on me and left their mark at The Post Office.

RIP, gentlemen, and thanks for the memories.

'Big Chris'

Chris was a man mountain, famously well-endowed, which he unashamedly showed off whenever we gave him grief. It was his way of saying, "Yeah, you can have a go, but I own this, so who's laughing now?" Funny stuff.

Chris was obsessed with achieving the perfect tan, though his motorbike helmet did not help as it had a visor to block the sun. Naturally, he removed it to sun himself. Most of us would lather up with sunscreen as a warm day out on delivery could fry a man to a crisp, but Chris wanted the bronzed Aussie look.

He always had a girlfriend, perhaps more than one at a time, and I will never forget a phone conversation he had with one at The Post Office. She had teased him about something he said, and he returned with, "Baby, I love you, you're all I think about!" before breaking into laughter. I think she had another go at him regarding his sincerity.

One day, Carlos imitated Chris by taking the visor off his own helmet and said, "Going out today with no visor, going to get burnt to a crisp, then try to pick up some chicks with my leathery face." It was light banter, nothing serious, but I remember laughing long and hard at that.

Chris was always short of money, constantly asking the office for loose change.

"You got a dollar, Dick?" (He called everyone 'Dick'). I wasn't sure why he always needed a dollar to get through the day, but he asked for one religiously. Looking back, I realised a dollar could buy a piece of carrot cake or a can of coke at a local deli, so it was enough to keep him going.

Later I discovered the reason. Chris lived on muesli flakes and little else while investing all his postie pay into a block of land where he kept a horse or two. That was his goal in life, which he achieved in a reasonably short time, thanks in part to his workmates giving him a dollar here and there until payday.

His nickname was obvious: 'Dollar Dick'. It had nothing to do with his anatomy, just a reflection of his habit of asking for a gold coin donation. To this day, I do not believe he ever repaid anyone. Chris is no longer with us, but he will always be a part of an office that somehow attracted characters like him.

RIP, big fella…

'Fearless Phil'

Looking back, I can honestly say with all sincerity that I didn't know Fearless Phil too well, but he was an absolute gentleman and would not have hurt a fly. In fact, no one had a bad word to say about him. Phil was as fit as an athlete, delivered his round on a pushbike and wore a distinctive pair of white running shoes, not unlike the great Freddy Mercury.

Phil weighed around 70 kg and owned the physique of a greyhound. He also owned a rather funny habit of 'showboating'. Back in the 90's, a postie earned a modest wage, but Phil would fill his tiny wallet with fifty-dollar notes and leave it on full display at the top of his sorting frame.

It was usually after pay day and would prompt comments from us like, "Must be pay week, Phil's wallet is overflowing again". (I think Phil deliberately chose the smallest wallet possible so he could show off his loot.)

Phil loved his music, and I recall one morning him bringing in a tape to play on our office stereo but unfortunately it only lasted around one song because he decided to switch the volume up a little too loud.

Ted came marching over, turned it off and told Phil, "If you can't listen to your music at a reasonable volume, try silence for the rest of the morning!"

Phil turned a shade of red, not unlike that of a rose in full bloom as his efforts to get the rest of us pumped up with some tunes took a nose-dive due to his over-enthusiasm with the volume.

Our office wasn't far from a busy local pub, and I can still envisage Phil one Friday afternoon after he finished his round, dressed like John Travolta from the 80's hit "Staying Alive", complete with a silk shirt and black pants. He was heading out for a big night as he loved the social scene.

Phil passed away several years ago but will always be remembered as a bloody good postie, a member of the much-maligned Breakfast Club and a bloke who did his job with a minimum of fuss.

RIP Phil, thanks for the memories.

'KG'

I once lived in a shared house not far from work with four other people. One of the girls went on holiday, met KG, a German fellow, brought him back to Australia, married him, and they had two kids over the following years.

Back in the day, as I may have already explained in this book, most jobs were found through word of mouth rather than scanning the employment section of the paper. Workforce organisations were basically non-existent. That's how many employees were found; someone would recommend a person if a position came up at their workplace, rather than going through the long, tedious process of hiring.

I knew KG needed an income, as his wife had to take time off work to raise the kids, and I knew he would jump at the chance for a position. I mentioned him to my team leader, and he was given a start.

KG took to it like a duck to water. He was simply brilliant at his job, no fuss, didn't talk too much unlike the rest of us, and he was possibly the politest postie I had ever met. Even though it was a long time ago, I can still remember Carlos shouting one morning during sorting, "KG, you are a revelation to this office!"

I'm not sure what KG did to make Carlos so happy, but I remember feeling chuffed because you always want someone you've recommended for a job to fit in. And he did. Everyone liked KG.

He worked at The Post Office for perhaps two or three years before applying for a position about an hour out of the city. He and his family were looking to escape the big smoke and start a new chapter.

I lost contact with KG, as social media was not around back then, and sometimes it's just a fact of life that you lose touch with people. I received sad news several years ago that KG had passed away after a long illness, and it hit me hard.

He was in the prime of his life, perhaps in his mid-40s. KG was the sort of guy you would never speak ill of. And while that term can often be used loosely, it certainly wasn't the case with him. Just a top bloke.

KG, I hope you, Phil, and Big Chris are looking after each other up there. RIP buddy. You made the postie grade in another country, and then some.

The Reunion, November 2020

To be honest, I didn't recognise Larry when he walked into a Perth pub in November 2020. We had organized to meet after twenty something years of very little contact whatsoever; perhaps just an occasional email.

In fact, Larry walked straight past me as I was watching some footy highlights on the big screen. We glanced at each other briefly before he moved into another section of the pub.

I thought to myself, *Was that Larry? Nah, Larry had a huge curly mop of hair last time I saw him at The Post Office in the 90s. Hang on, it's been twenty-something years. That could have been Larry.*

I sent him a text:

"Larry, it's GT. I'm watching the footy on the big screen. Look for a bloke wearing blue jeans and a blue top with grey hair and a silly grin."

Sure enough, Larry walked back in, a bit less hair than in the 90's, yet still impressive for a man of 67, with sideburns a 70's porn star would have been proud of.

"GT, how the hell are ya mate?! How long has it been, twenty years?!"

"I think you're right, Larry, all of twenty, closer to twenty-two. You're still looking a million bucks, buddy!"

We talked non-stop for at least an hour. Well, that's not quite right. Larry talked non-stop for over an hour, and I struggled to get a word in as he dazzled me with hilarious postal stories from his thirty-something years in the game.

Then Oggy turned up.

"Hey Larry, I reckon that's Oggy."

Larry glanced over, got up, and yelled for the entire pub to hear:

"OGGY, YA BOOFHEAD, OVER HERE!"

Seriously, Larry had not changed a bit from the first day he walked into The Post Office in the early 90's, full of bad manners, bravado, and more bad manners. Whether in a pub or a post office, a crowd never stopped Larry from telling someone exactly what he thought about them, loudly and in jest. It was just how he behaved back then.

A beer or two later, Oggy said, "I'm retiring in two weeks, having a send-off. You blokes coming?"

Larry and I both said yes, and we kept our word. Two weeks later, we met for a drink and a chat about the good old days. Oggy, Larry, Leapy, Kenny, Eli, and I all reunited for the first time since the late 90's, some 22 years on.

A lot of stories were shared as the beers flowed. Oggy looked back on a postie career spanning about 40 years. We had all been part of a small team at a northern suburbs postal outlet in Perth, WA, chasing dogs, delivering mail on pushbikes and Honda 110's, and usually finishing our rounds just after lunch.

Thanks for the good times, fellas.

Chapter 14:
Complaints, Junk Mail, The Mail Sorting Fairy

The Complaints File

To say I had a complaints file as long as my arm would be a stretch, but over twenty-something years, I did accrue a query or two from a customer or three. My most memorable one involved someone who made a rather funny complaint about their postie, me, disrespecting their dog.

Yes, you read that correctly.

I was called into the office one morning by the boss, who explained a complaint from a customer who was upset about how I had *barked* at her dog. I raised my eyebrows as I read the printed transcript emailed to Oz Post management with a 'please explain' request.

I explained it as best I could without breaking into laughter. My boss was just doing his job, but I struggled to take it seriously.

"OK Boss, from memory, it was like this. I did have a few words with the dog in question, but it was all a bit of fun. Anyhow, why can't I bark at a dog if he barks at me first? I mean, c'mon, he started it!"

The boss didn't respond; he just looked at me like a confused puppy dog, as I mentioned elsewhere in this book.

I then did my best to describe the incident:

"Yeah, yeah, settle down and woof, woof, to you too buddy. That was it, Boss. That's all I said, or rather, woofed. Word for word, or is that woof for woof?"

The boss however didn't see the funny side of my attempted humour to lighten the moment.

"OK GT, I will send your version of events to head office and leave it at that. Can you make sure you don't bark at her dog again, thanks?"

"No wuz, Boss. Trust me, my days of barking at dogs are over."

I walked out of the office shaking my head, thinking if this went to court, my lawyer would surely get me off on a technicality. I don't actually own a bark, and that alone would have had my case thrown out. Funny stuff indeed.

There was one other complaint involving a dog, just as silly. During my postie career, I took on a couple of lawn-mowing jobs that came about through parcel deliveries. After getting to know some customers, I offered to mow their lawns as a few were elderly. I didn't charge much and usually did the mowing on weekends.

At one address, I ended up mowing the neighbour's lawn too. They had a dog that liked me, so I regularly threw a ball or gave it a tummy scratch. Eventually, they moved house, and I stumbled across their new place by accident. The dog came out to say hello, and I gave her the usual tummy rub. The owner didn't recognise me and phoned a complaint: "The postie was stirring up my dog!"

I explained it all to the boss later that same day as he quizzed me about my 'stirring'. Safe to say that after that episode, I left the dog alone, for fear of another complaint being phoned through.

I sometimes wonder if my old workplace still has my complaints file and whether it could be accessed, just for nostalgia's sake. I also wonder whether those complaints would ever be held against me if I decided to make a comeback to the industry. If nothing else, it would make an entertaining read.

Most of the complaints I received over the years were ones I could talk my way out of, as I've been told on more than one occasion that I am a very good bullshit artist. Some complaints, however, required me to admit defeat, like when I accidentally delivered an item to the wrong address.

One incident stands out where I bore the cost of the missing item myself.

One morning, I received a notification about a parcel I had misdelivered. When I retraced my steps from the previous day, I realised I had placed a non-signature item at the correct house number, but the wrong street. Bright spark.

I knocked on the customer's door and asked the obvious question:

"Hi there, sincere apologies, but I left a parcel behind your pot plant at the front door yesterday that was meant for the next street. Do you have it?"

"Sorry, we don't have it," came the reply.

I may have been in my early 50s at the time, but my memory was fine. I immediately put two and two together, got five, and realised that this customer may have thought a free pair of shoes, the contents of the misdelivered parcel, was too good to pass up.

On to plan B. I drove to the next street, knocked on the door of the person who should have received the parcel, and apologised profusely. I asked what the item was, prepared to cover it myself if it wasn't too expensive.

It was a $67 pair of shoes. To avoid any drama, I decided to pay. I took her bank details and transferred the $67 that night. I didn't have to, but it was my mistake, and I didn't believe anyone else should pay for it. A couple of hours' pay later, the matter was resolved.

I learned two things from that mishap.

1. Going a little slower and saying the street name either to myself or even out loud as I turned into it would have prevented the mistake, just as I found out early on in my career when I delivered the mail to the wrong street.

2. People are always on the lookout for a bargain. If one turns up on their doorstep by mistake, it may be too good to pass up.

And what did I tell the boss?

Simply that I had retrieved the parcel and delivered it to the correct household. Sometimes, to save grief and paperwork, it's easier to handle things yourself, even if it costs the equivalent of a carton of beer.

Looking back, I probably should have let the insurance take care of it. But sometimes it's easier to man up, take it on the chin, and accept the consequences of a mistake. Plus, I saved the customer and management some time and paperwork.

We live and we learn. I'm certain I have written that more than once in this book.

Junk Mail

There isn't a business anywhere in the world where management would consider their own leaflets or pamphlets as junk. So, I still wonder why JUNK MAIL stickers are used on letterboxes.

If I were promoting my own business with leaflet drops, I would ignore every single JUNK MAIL sticker. I wouldn't consider my material as junk; I would see it as advertising.

There are three main types of stickers, and possibly a fourth, to look out for when delivering:

- NO JUNK MAIL

- NO ADVERTISING MATERIAL

- NO CIRCULARS

There's another I have seen from time to time that should be an absolute must for refusing flyers:

- NO JUNK MAIL, NO ADVERTISING MATERIAL, NO CIRCULARS, NO EXCEPTIONS

I believe there is a company online that can create a custom sticker covering all your requirements for advertising material. One minor issue: it won't stop political advertising, because the government requires their election material to be delivered to every letterbox. No exceptions.

So, if you are one of those customers who thought that you had found something either online or elsewhere that you could stick on your letterbox that would make your house exempt from advertising material or junk mail, think again.

If you don't want anything in your letterbox other than addressed items, try the 'no exceptions' sticker. It will stop most advertising, though you cannot prevent election material. Remember, there are always loopholes, and some institutions aren't interested in what the 'common person' says.

As for sticker placement, here are a few tips:

- Put it on the front of the letterbox.

- Don't place the sticker either under the lid of the letterbox or to the side of it because of the obvious; it can save the delivery person some time if they can spot a sticker from the road.

- Make the sticker large enough to be seen easily.

I am all for surprises but nothing used to piss me off more than riding into someone's driveway to deliver some junk mail only to find a sticker under the lid or to the side of it.

Surprise!!

Yep, brilliant, thanks for that...

I remember a comical incident on motorbike deliveries. I rode up to a block of units and was confronted by a gentleman in a dressing gown and slippers.

As I approached, I offered a polite, "G'day mate." He replied, "I don't want any junk mail in number 5."

"No worries, mate," I said.

I got off the bike, grabbed some pamphlets, and delivered them to all the letterboxes except for those with a NO JUNK MAIL sticker. The dressing gown guy watched closely to ensure number 5 received nothing.

As I rode off, he grabbed something from his letterbox, waved it at me, and started yelling something I couldn't understand as I shifted into second gear. I just waved back. I wasn't interested in arguing with a guy in a dressing gown early in the morning, especially as I had followed his instructions twice (once verbally, and once again by the sticker on his letterbox).

My theory was that he hadn't checked his letterbox the previous afternoon or morning. That's plenty of time for someone to drop something in that they don't classify as junk, regardless of a sticker.

So, when I arrived around 9 am, he thought I was his first delivery. But considering the number of other delivery organisations out there nowadays, I may have been his third delivery in the space of 14 hours if he had decided to tuck himself into bed around 7 pm.

Moral of the story? Follow the signs and don't ignore no junk mail or no advertising stickers. Otherwise, you might be confronted by a man in a dressing gown early in the morning who is looking for an argument.

Just another Kurt thing

I will never forget back in the 90's at The Post Office where Kurt was always looking for ways to avoid delivering too many flyers on his round. He wanted a part-time job rather than a full-time one, and if he could get home early most days, he would find a way.

So, he spoke to as many customers as he could on his round and asked if they would like a *no junk mail* sticker. Almost all of them said yes.

From memory, they cost around 50 cents or a dollar each. Kurt would collect the money, buy a bulk amount of stickers, and as he delivered their mail, he would stick them on the letterboxes. This effectively covered about half of his delivery round. Brilliant.

Kurt was a little unusual in most aspects of life, not just mail delivery.

Picture this: for those unfamiliar with mail rounds, there was nothing worse than cruising along on a quiet day and having to stop to deliver advertising material to letterboxes without stickers. Considering most rounds had between 1,000 and 1,500 delivery points, skipping half of them made for a happy day.

Another flyer that had to be delivered, of course, was the street verge collection flyer. For anyone wanting to get rid of excess junk, whether green waste or household items, the free verge collection day was a must, so that flyer went to every household.

There you go, the advertising material industry explained. A complete pain for a postie but a necessity for businesses to get their products out there.

As a customer, apart from election flyers, it's all about how clever you are when choosing a sticker for your letterbox as to what you may or may not receive as far as flyers are concerned.

The 'Mail Sorting Fairy'

Believe it or not, there is no such thing as the 'Mail Sorting Fairy', the one who magically puts delivery rounds together for each postie overnight. I was probably called something similar by the guys at The Post Office all those years back, and that was one of the more polite things I was called.

In all seriousness, it's like the Tooth Fairy. We all like to believe it exists, but I hate to break it to you…

No one really cares how a letter or article is sorted, as long as it ends up in the correct letterbox or behind the pot plant next to the front door. Personally, I was amazed at the sorting process when I started as a postie. There was a rawness to it that relied on a slight bit of genius, despite the simplicity of it.

In the first edition of this book, I explained the entire sorting process, and it was an absolute head wreck of epic proportions. After writing it, I swore I would never do it again, as interesting as it was. I will give a shortened version here, though even that is tricky due to the complexity.

I had no idea how a letter ended up in my letterbox. I assumed the process was simple and maybe a machine put it in order for the postie, or the mail sorting fairy did it during the night. I could not have been further from the truth.

If I were to simplify it, I could tell you to read the next two paragraphs and skip the rest. But if you want a challenge, read the entire explanation and try to make sense of it.

Back in the day, every postie had a literal hand in distributing every letter and oversized article (OA) dropped off at the mail distribution centre in the early hours. Each postie had to learn where every single item needed to go, a giant jigsaw puzzle.

Our office had 10 delivery rounds. During the primary sorting phase each morning, we individually sorted anywhere from 500 to 600 letters on a quiet day, around two trays, to 1,500 letters on a busy day, five or six trays. Each tray held roughly 200 to 300 letters, depending on size and thickness.

The process could take up to four hours, especially after a long weekend with huge volumes. There was no sequence to the mail when it arrived; it was up to us to manually sort it to where it needed to go.

I recently spoke with my old team leader, Leapy, who handled mail statistics. He said a tray could hold up to 330 letters, but for simplicity, I have rounded it down to 300.

In the 90s, letters were the main form of communication, whether utility bills or personal letters, long before emails existed.

We sorted letters into numbered pigeonholes for each delivery round (1-10). Learning which letter went to which round took time. Our 10 rounds might have serviced between 250 and 300 streets combined.

In layman's terms, every postie had to memorise up to 300 streets and which delivery round a letter belonged to during the initial sorting phase.

We then moved to the OA section, sorting larger items into numbered baskets on wheels that could be moved next to the sorting bays. On a busy day, these three-foot-high, two-foot-wide baskets would fill quickly. We would grab handfuls of articles, place them in containers, and take them to the correct bay.

Looking back, the system worked efficiently on light to moderate days, but struggled on high-volume days. Some streets were split between delivery rounds, adding to the complexity. For example, 'Zen Street' might be split: Round 1 delivered 1-100, Round 7 delivered 101-200.

Every sorting frame had a street index attached to the top. I will never forget looking up at it the first time and how daunted I was at the task that lay ahead, yet within a few months, I rarely had to look up at it as I had memorized the lot.

We did, however, have to pass a sorting test. From memory, it was 25 letters per minute, and 20 oversized articles per minute. On busy utility bill days, a round might receive five or six trays of bills plus another five trays of primary sorted mail, around 10 trays total, up to 3,000 letters. Sometimes both Western Power and Telstra bills arrived together, and rates bills a couple of times a year. Some houses would have three utility bills at once.

Magazines and A4-sized envelopes (oversized articles) came through in large volumes, sometimes 15 to 20 bundles per round, with 15 to 30 items per bundle depending on thickness. This was why the old Hondas had two carriers, one for letters and one for oversized articles.

Once the initial phase of primary sorting was completed and the mail was allocated to each delivery round, a postie would stand in front of their alphabetically labelled sorting frame and basically just follow the alphabet. 'Zen Street' would obviously be on the bottom row, 'Mason Street' would be somewhere in the middle, and 'Alpha Street' would of course be on the top row.

The frames, however, were not arranged in delivery order. Once all the letters were placed into the pigeonholes, a little red book was required which explained the delivery sequence. For example, 'Zen Street' might have been the very last pigeonhole in the sorting frame, yet it could have been the first street in the delivery sequence. After about two to three weeks of checking the little red book daily, the delivery order eventually became embedded in memory, and the book was no longer needed.

Letters were usually sorted first, and a postie could then sit down to put the round together. If there was a long street, for instance 1-100, a postie would break the letters into 10's, 20's, 30's etc in the bottom row of pigeonholes initially, before sorting them precisely in order in between the fingers on the left hand which acted as dividers.

A street could vary in sequence, but usually it was odds first, 1-99, then evens, 100-2, as an example.

If you have seen a photo or even watched the movie *Edward Scissorhands*, that was what your left hand looked like during delivery order sorting. Bundles of letters were bound with elastic bands and numbered in delivery order. Oversized articles were sorted in the bottom row of the pigeonholes, because they were too large to sort by hand, and then bundled and numbered.

A postie was not permitted to load the Honda more than a certain weight as there was a weight limit to follow (although some guys gave it a reasonable nudge regardless). Secure relay points were set up to pick up more mail once the bike was empty.

Looking back, the entire process of primary sorting, learning to sort your own round into the alphabetically labelled frames, and memorising the delivery order probably took around three months, with the majority of that time dedicated to the primary sorting phase.

There was no online shopping back then, at least not to the extent of today. Most of what we delivered were letters, oversized envelopes, and many magazines, which do not get delivered as often nowadays apart from RAC information items. A few bundles of those alone could quickly bring a postie bike to the weight limit.

Delivery time for a round on a Honda 110 averaged out at around two to two and a half hours and perhaps three to three and a half hours on a busy day. Pushbike rounds usually took three to four hours on average and some days were a hard slog in wet weather.

Nowadays, the changes are huge, and apart from the massive drop in letter volume, which has more than halved, delivery times have doubled. The reason, of course, is simple; a postie is now basically a courier with a scanner who may scan up to 150 items on a busy day and perhaps closer to 200 on a high-volume day over the Xmas delivery period.

A postie today has to be a Tetris expert. Sorting, bundling, and delivering dozens of items of different shapes that all need an initial scan, then a scan on delivery, perhaps a card if the customer isn't home, and more scanning when the item is returned to the office, is a serious time consumer. A six-hour delivery day is not uncommon.

Alphabet pigeonholes are basically a thing of the past, though they may still exist in smaller country towns where mail and product volumes are lower. Most delivery rounds now use three individually addressed sorting frames sequenced in delivery order, and most delivery centres receive mail already sequenced.

Night sorters now take care of any items that aren't sorted by the sequencing process, leaving the postie to focus on the Tetris style sorting system that can test their patience on any given day, especially at Christmas.

Electric vehicles are slowly taking over most delivery rounds across Australia. However, depending on terrain, volume, or both, some towns, suburbs, or even cities still use the Honda 110 as the main delivery vehicle.

So, there you have it. I may have missed some details, but this I hope gives a bit of insight into how mail sorting and delivery has evolved over the years. The 'Mail Sorting Fairy' definitely does not exist, though give the new technology a few more years and it will probably be unrecognisable from today, and that fairy may just make an appearance after all.

I often reminisce with some fellow retired postie mates over an ale or two about days gone by when the entire postie gig was perhaps a little less complicated than today.

Personally, give me back the old Honda 110, letters as the predominant source of delivery, a two-and-a-half-hour delivery round with an average finishing time of 1pm, a regular game of golf with my old postie mates and I would happily return full time to the industry.

Dream on buddy....

The 'Best Mate' Customer

A few years back, I started delivering parcels to a gentleman who treated me like a long-lost mate from day one. Each delivery turned into an epic chat about life, AFL matches, his marriage, and mostly, what he had ordered online.

Let me clarify: he did the talking, I did the listening.

As his postie, it was part of the job to hear about his orders, the bargains he had found, the prices he had paid, and how he had bartered the seller down to an acceptable price.

That customer was an absolute ripper, and he was not an isolated case. I regularly delivered to another gentleman who collected replica toy cars. Each delivery was met with the same excitement: "Hey GT, wait while I open the parcel, you will love this." I even got a guided tour of his trophy room, which he called his 'superannuation room of goodies'.

I was not just his postie; I had become his new best mate, perhaps showing more interest in his hobby than his wife did.

One of my all-time favourite customers was a happily married woman who was a friend of a friend. She was one of the funniest people I have ever delivered to. Some of our conversations could have made a podcast with a regular audience. Sometimes I would call in just to say g'day, even when her business had no deliveries, just to have a chat.

I learned early in my career that a postie can brighten someone's day with or without a delivery. Often it was more about the social interaction, having someone impartial to talk to, bounce ideas off, or vent frustration to.

I realised from day one that the postie's wage was not going to make me rich, but it guaranteed an entertaining work life. Customers brightened my day as much as I brightened theirs, some more so than others…

Chapter 15:
Hysteria, Bits n Bobs,
In Conclusion

Hysteria

Have you ever had one of those moments in life, particularly in your chosen profession, when you took a brief moment to pat yourself on the back and think: Yep, I've made it…?

Well, that happened to me towards the end of my days as a postie while I was cruising along delivering parcels on the south coast of WA. It was one of those days where the sun was shining, the birds were singing, and I thought to myself, life is pretty good.

We had a local DJ by the name of Wazza, an absolute legend of local radio, who loved his music, particularly glam rock. He was from my era of music: the 70s, 80s, and maybe even the early 90s before grunge came along and briefly messed it all up.

Anyone who has spent an hour or two with me will know that my favourite song of all time is "Hysteria" by Def Leppard, an absolute glam rock masterpiece of a ballad, and a song that I told my kids: either play it at my funeral, or I will haunt you. True story.

At the time I was delivering, I think I had either misplaced my precious iPod shuffle or there was an issue hooking it up to the van stereo. So I did what any old dinosaur would do when they wanted to hear a song: I messaged the local DJ and put in a request.

It took me on another trip down memory lane. When I was a kid in the early 80s, we used to have a local Friday night radio request show. Anyone could ring up and request a song for themselves or perhaps their boyfriend or girlfriend. I swear Wazza was the DJ back then. If he wasn't, he was certainly not far off starting the gig, as he was a long-time stalwart of local radio on the south coast who has since retired.

Wazza was brilliant, an absolute gentleman, always happy to keep the locals entertained with requests and plenty of glam rock. I am uncertain of exactly how the conversation went, but my request for "Hysteria" was honoured around 9 am one sunny morning. I still remember the location to this day because it was one of those feel-good moments you look back on with pride.

"And here's a song for our local postie, GT, who is out there delivering parcels on the south coast: Hysteria by Def Leppard."

"I gotta know tonight, if you're alone tonight..." and I sang every word loud and proud.

Wazza, if you ever read this book, thanks mate, not only for the "Hysteria" request that day but for being the greatest local DJ the south coast of WA has ever produced. Keep on rocking, buddy.

A Few Bits 'n Bobs

The Whistle

I only just recently learned that posties used to carry a whistle with them on their pushbikes and that they used to blow the whistle to alert the customer that their mail had arrived. By all reports, the system was abolished around 1980 due to the issues that it caused with dogs, which should be rather obvious, it drove them nuts.

Perhaps that's why dogs used to chase posties. Looking back, the idea of blowing a whistle was possibly the worst thing a postie could do because it alerted dogs that a potential victim was at the front letterbox and 'in need' of being chased. Thank goodness the idea was discarded long before I started my career.

Perks of the Job

I worked in an era of small postal outlets, before larger delivery centres were built where three or four suburbs were combined and around forty posties all worked together. The Post Office owned a tiny shed, and it was always a battle to fit all the pushbikes and motorcycles inside. Management came up with a masterstroke and asked if posties would like to take their 'work vehicle' home at the end of the day.

I accepted with glee and for two or three years, I rode the Honda 110 to work, delivered my round, then occasionally stopped in at the local supermarket on the way home to buy groceries. The perks of being a postie in the 90s, working at an office too small to store the vehicles, are still fond memories. The fuel I saved over those years was enough to fund an annual holiday.

F... ups

Over my career as a postie, apart from delivering to the wrong street early on, I vividly remember two incidents in the work van as a parcel delivery driver that I would definitely class as 'f... ups' of reasonably large proportions.

The first happened when I failed to close the passenger door properly before leaving the work shed. At the first roundabout, just a few hundred metres from work, the door opened and five or six parcels on the front seat fell onto the road. Luckily, none contained glass or fragile items. I picked them up with minimal disruption to other motorists and carried on with deliveries. From that day on, I always ensured the passenger door was shut properly.

The other incident involved the front section of the work van becoming completely detached. I was reversing out of a tricky driveway when the front bumper got caught on a hedge. I didn't notice at first, so I kept reversing, and the entire front bumper fell off. I suspect it had not been attached properly in the first place, or another driver had loosened it somehow. Either way, I was left with a completely removed front section to reattach.

I picked up the pieces, drove back home, a five-minute drive, grabbed a drill and some cable ties, made a few adjustments, and reattached the bumper. No one noticed a thing. It was a work of art from someone who usually failed metalwork and woodwork at school, but on this occasion, I passed the ultimate test and truly thought outside the square.

A Pommy Postie's point of View

I had almost finished this book when I stumbled across a post online by a UK postie. I felt it was worth sharing. The similarities between posties on either side of the world are striking, particularly regarding letterboxes and naked customers.

FJTW, a postie from the UK, wrote:

"Things we like about customers: have a letterbox that works, doesn't have sharp pointy things inside it, and if you get a lot of parcels, maybe some kind of container to put them in would be nice. Make sure we have a clear path to your letterbox so we don't brush against wet bushes. Just be nice to us, we are delivering the stuff you ordered. A simple 'thank you' can brighten a bad day. If you have a wall-mounted external letterbox, make sure letters can actually go in. The cheap Argos/Ebay ones are rubbish and can cut our fingers.

I've seen pretty much everything. A mix of naked men and women, some on purpose, many by accident.

Also, we spot the packaging for LoveHoney and Ann Summers. WE KNOW WHEN YOU BUY SEX TOYS. THEY SAY DISCREET PACKAGING? RUBBISH. 100........Road, Bath, UK, in a long thin box? We know. We usually have a giggle and carry on. Pensioners buy a lot of sex toys. I guess what else is there to do once you retire? Just imagine knowing that Ethel down the road had a shelf full of dongs.

Anything people want to know, just ask. I love the job and am proud to be a postman."

That was our English Postie talking about his job in the UK.

P.s, I had to blank the name of the road out, hence the dots. (This bloke sounds a bit like Larry and something he would write.) Not sure of their privacy policy in the UK however 'FJTW' has posted this information and included the address of a customer who apparently buys sex toys. Not sure whether this guy is still a postie; it was written 4 years ago. ('LoveHoney' and 'Anne Summers' are apparently the names of two adult 'intimate apparel' companies.)

Sounds like 'FJTW' could have fitted right in with the rest of us at The Post Office in the Land of Oz. We may have just got him to leave out customer addresses if ever he went public with his postie views and experiences...

In Conclusion

My days of sorting and delivering mail at The Post Office in the 90s gave me a view of the postal industry that I am forever grateful for. It's like anything in life; we often take something for granted until we understand the intricacies of it all.

When I used to see the postie ride up and down our street, I had no idea how a letter for my house ended up in the correct order for delivery. After learning the ins and outs of the job, I realised there was a lot more to the process than I could have imagined. I consider myself fortunate not only to have secured a position in the postal industry for as long as I did, but even more so at an office that inspired me to write this book.

The guys I worked with at The Post Office, and their individual quirks, were something out of a comedy movie script. Learning the trade with their help and humour made most days outrageously enjoyable.

To Leapy, Carlos, Kenny, Eli, Hammy, Kurt, Burns, Thorney, Kel, Bog, Larry, Col, and Pardo (the graffiti artist), thanks for the inspiration, and I hope I have done you guys proud. We used to call ourselves the *A Team*, or as Carlos once stated, *The Hawthorn of the 80s.*

To KG, Fearless Phil, and Big Chris, you will be forever remembered as part of the *A Team* at The Post Office. Well played and thanks for the memories.

Rip Gentlemen.

The older generation postie who is still in the system and has seen some outrageous changes over the decades may look back on the days of alphabetical pigeonhole sorting frames, and the setting up of mail between the fingers, as a time to cherish for its simplicity and rawness.

On the other side of the coin, the new generation postie might welcome that old-school process with open arms, or perhaps frown upon it as prehistoric. Explaining today's mail processing, with sequenced mail and individually addressed sorting frames, to a retired postie from days gone by would be like explaining to a kid nowadays that in the AFL, a team used to regularly kick 20-plus goals to win a game.

Both generations have experienced completely different ways of doing the job. There are pros and cons to both systems, which management can ponder for the future of the industry. Every now and then a whisper may be heard that the old sorting frames, due to the size of the pigeonholes may just be the way to go in the future due to the online shopping craze that will only grow in the years to come; along with the endless number of scannable items that come through the system on a daily basis that a postie has to sort into order as best they can.

Did the old system have it right, or is the new system head and shoulders above it? Time will tell.

I resigned from my position as a parcel delivery officer in early 2022 to try something else because, to be honest, I was a little worn out from running parcels to front doorsteps and keeping up with increasing volumes. Plus, it was never the same as the old gig, despite working for the same company.

I miss the days on a Honda 110 that took me half the time to deliver compared to today and I miss playing golf with my fellow workmates at around 1pm once or twice a week after we had finished our rounds.

I also miss the customer interaction; the good the bad and the ugly, that I have written fondly about in this book.

By the way, for you newbies, *The Good, The Bad and The Ugly* was a western movie from the 70's. Yep I am getting old.

A smile on a customer's face, particularly a kid's, when a deadline such as Christmas or a birthday was met, made the job worthwhile. Customers who told me that I had made their day, or even their week, with a delivery they were relying on, made me believe that what I was doing was a unique type of job. You know, a win/win scenario.

I always looked forward to seeing *Mrs Smith* and cringed at getting a complaint from *Karen*, yet both customers gave me the chance to excel as a postie, perhaps in different ways. *Mrs Smith* will always be a joy to deliver to and should inspire each and every postie to strive for perfection because basically she's just a nice human being.

Keeping Karen happy, however is a tough gig but should be a challenge all posties should accept and if I may offer once again a small piece of advice it would be this: Even if there is just a one percent chance that she may be home, knock on the door anyhow as it may save you from being uploaded to a social media platform or YouTube.

Just like a surfer searching for the perfect wave, a postie can also ride a barrel of perfection on any day if it all falls into place. It usually starts with good sorting.

Van contract parcel deliveries in my final seven years in the postal industry were a little less complicated than mail sorting and delivery. On a wet and windy day, when I used to see the postie ride past me on a motorcycle, rugged up in wet weather gear, I welcomed the warmth of a heater and the sound of a radio or iPod. Arguing over a radio station feels like a lifetime ago, and Def Leppard received a daily burst without anyone complaining about my taste in music.

So, is there anything I would like to leave as a parting gesture to the postal industry? Hey, I did my best! I was however just one of thousands of posties in the land of Oz, and nothing I did was out of the ordinary apart from owning a silly memory for names, numbers and situations that I felt deserved to go down in postal history.

For the three or four of you who read this book, you now know a whole lot more about the postal industry, particularly the sorting side of the job.

A postie, whether on a bike, in a van, or on foot, is in a unique position. They are their own boss once out on the road and can manage deliveries however they like, as long as the customer receives their goods.

In most cases, as long as the customer gets what they ordered, everyone is happy.

Admittedly, I got myself into a bit of strife over the years with shortcuts and certain delivery methods that wouldn't exactly be classed as 'by the book'. However, I usually only ever got quizzed by management, not the customer.

The other appealing aspect of being a postie is this: if you have a bit of experience under your belt, you can turn up at any postal outlet in Australia and probably find yourself employment, as I did on a recent trip to the Sunshine Coast in Queensland.

I planned on staying a few weeks with a mate, which ended up being a three-month working holiday after I got chatting one day with the local postie who was in charge of the contract for the area. He offered me a job. The postie job can literally take you places.

For any posties out there, who have read this book, or any potential future posties looking to make a career out of delivering items, I will leave you with that one piece of advice that the delivery Zen Master gave me all those years ago, and will leave it up to you as to whether or not you believe the job is worth pursuing:

"Remember guys and girls, when the postie delivers up and down the streets of suburbia, it's a sign to many that everything is still OK in the world".

Aah yes, the simple things in life...

Glenn Thompson (GT)

glennthompson@westnet.com.au

Glenn Thompson

Acknowledgements

My dear old Mum and Dad left a legacy of sorts when they passed, and I suppose I felt it necessary to leave one myself. After all, you get one shot at life and perhaps one chance to leave your mark on the world, so why not do something that your kids and grandkids can have a beer and a laugh over when you are long gone?

Dad (Alf) is part of the Goldfields history of Western Australia. It all started innocently in 1980 when he stumbled across an old grave at Hawks Nest, not far from Laverton, while prospecting for gold (which he found). He tidied up the grave, which turned out to belong to a young New Zealand gold prospector, Jonny Aspinall, who had died from a lightning strike in 1896.

Dad wrote a book titled *And Some Found Graves*, detailing the history of the find, which led to both Mum and Dad visiting Jonny's relatives in New Zealand almost 100 years after his untimely death. It's a fascinating story and one Dad was proud to bring to life. His wish to have his ashes buried with Mum and also scattered on Jonny's grave was honoured in 2025.

Dad's local golfing heroics, he was the best player in Albany in the mid to late 70s, with a handicap of 0, or 'scratch', and a club championship win in 1977, paled in comparison to the goldfields legacy he left, but boy could he hit a golf ball beautifully.

Mum (Glenis) never wrote a book, but she spent her life writing, particularly to friends. She never typed a letter despite being a schoolteacher for over 30 years; she just loved writing, perhaps a Thompson trait. Mum's legacy can be traced back to her teaching days and would regularly play out on her supermarket shopping days in Albany (which I witnessed from time to time) when former students would stop her and thank her for being their 'favourite primary school teacher'.

Mum and Dad both left their legacies, inspiring me to do the same. Dad always called me 'Fred'. Still not sure why, but I look back on it with a smile.

As for 'Fred's' legacy: I have only been good at three things in life, if I may be brutally honest; writing, delivering stuff, and hitting tennis balls, which eventually led me to teaching tennis as a way to make a living. Coaching led to my first book, *Perspective, A Tennis Point of View*, published in 2019. For some reason, I have felt compelled to write books about things I am passionate about.

Writing this book would never have been possible if it weren't for Ted, Leapy and another fellow who I haven't mentioned up until this point yet was responsible for my 'rebirth' as a postie.

'Robbo', the postal manager on the south coast, offered me a position after I initially left the job in Perth, tried something else and then realised that the grass wasn't greener on the other side. Robbo slotted me into his team which ultimately extended my postie career by another 15 years.

Thanks Robbo, champion.

I have previously mentioned before that I loved the hours that the postie gig offered, as it allowed me to manage the day-to-day duties of shared parenting.

Thanks to Mum, on the weeks that I had the kids, I would basically high five her on the way out of the driveway at 5.45 am, go into work, sort the mail for my round then return home to take the kids to school.

Mum did all the hard work like wake them up, give them brekky and made sure their school uniforms etc were the right way around. I would then take them to school, then go and deliver my postie round.

I never missed a sports day for any of my kids. I would get the program the day before, note the approximate times, and plan my deliveries around the races. The ability to deliver my round, take five or ten minutes to watch a race, and then continue deliveries over the course of the sports day was something few working parents could do, and I was forever grateful for that freedom.

(Not sure if management were ever aware of my movements on those days which probably looked like the local postie was having trouble with his directions, but I guess that it's like anything in life; as long as the job gets done, everyone is happy, particularly management.)

That was the job in a nutshell; freedom, the luxury of being your own boss, providing your skill set was up to scratch. It was like putting together a jigsaw puzzle in stages, always making sure the final piece was delivered, literally.

Nowadays, most postie bikes are monitored, mainly for safety, so parking a bike at a local school six or seven times over the course of a kids' sporting day may not be the smartest thing to do if you want to stay on the good side of management.

And finally, to my three kids. Just in case someone wants to sue me for any of the content in this book, I will simply refer to them as 'Amy', 'Kyle' and 'Cody'. They are all grown up now, which means one thing: I am getting older. I look back on those days of the early morning madness every second week when I had the kids as challenging yet rewarding. Most days, I was able to pick them up after school, grab a snack from Macca's, kick a footy at the park, take them to sports training or go to the beach, just 150 metres from our beach shack.

Mum filled in the rest of the gaps, bless her. Life was pretty good, all things considered.

I am forever grateful to the postie job for allowing me to have a life outside work, time with my kids, and to attend the occasional school sports carnival during work hours.

To Mum, Dad, Amy, Kyle, and Cody: thanks for inspiring me to write this book.

Love, 'Fred' (Dad)